Maryfield Academy

HARRINGTON PARK PRESS
Alice Street Editions
Judith P. Stelboum
Editor in Chief

Past Perfect by Judith P. Stelboum

Inside Out by Juliet Carrera

Facades by Alex Marcoux

Weeding at Dawn: A Lesbian Country Life by Hawk Madrone

His Hands, His Tools, His Sex, His Dress: Lesbian Writers on Their Fathers edited by Catherine Reid and Holly K. Iglesias

Treat by Angie Vicars

Yin Fire by Alexandra Grilikhes

From Flitch to Ash: A Musing on Trees and Carving by Diane Derrick

To the Edge by Cameron Abbott

Back to Salem by Alex Marcoux

Extraordinary Couples, Ordinary Lives by Lynn Haley-Banez and Joanne Garrett

Cat Rising by Cynn Chadwick

Maryfield Academy by Carla Tomaso

Ginger's Fire by Maureen Brady

Maryfield Academy

Carla Tomaso

Alice Street Editions
Harrington Park Press®
An Imprint of The Haworth Press, Inc.
New York • London • Oxford

Published by

Alice Street Editions, Harrington Park Press®, an imprint of The Haworth Press, Inc., 10 Alice Street, Binghamton, NY 13904-1580.

PUBLISHER'S NOTE
This is a work of fiction. Names, characters, places, and incidents either are the products of the author's imagination or are used fictitiously, and any resemblance to actual persons, living or dead, business establishments, events, or locales, is entirely coincidental.

Cover design by Marylouise E. Doyle.

Library of Congress Cataloging-in-Publication Data

Tomaso, Carla.
    Maryfield Academy / Carla Tomaso
        p. cm.
    ISBN 1-56023-423-7 (alk. paper)—ISBN 1-56023-424-5 (softcover)
    1. Anonymous letters—Fiction. 2. Catholic schools—Fiction. 3. English teachers—Fiction.
4. Women teachers—Fiction. 5. Pedophilia—Fiction. I. Title.

PS3570.O4297 M36 2003
813'.54—dc21
                                                                2002071731

For Lee Howard
a great woman, friend, and supporter of writers,
especially me

Editor's Foreword

Alice Street Editions provides a voice for established as well as up-and-coming lesbian writers, reflecting the diversity of lesbian interests, ethnicities, ages, and class. This cutting-edge series of novels, memoirs, and nonfiction writing welcomes the opportunity to present controversial views, explore multicultural ideas, encourage debate, and inspire creativity from a variety of lesbian perspectives. Through enlightening, illuminating, and provocative writing, Alice Street Editions can make a significant contribution to the visibility and accessibility of lesbian writing and bring lesbian-focused writing to a wider audience. Recognizing our own desires and ideas in print is life sustaining, acknowledging the reality of who we are, as well as our place in the world, individually and collectively.

Judith P. Stelboum
Editor in Chief
Alice Street Editions

Acknowledgments

I would like to thank Judith Selboum, PhD, and all the staff at The Haworth Press for making the publication of *Maryfield Academy* such a pleasure; Tim Lewis for the beautiful cover painting of the school; Terry Wolverton for being such a fine workshop leader and inspiring role model; Georgia Davis, Sheila Traviss, and Sally Charette for adding so much to my writing life; Naomi Sekely for believing in me; and finally, Mary Hayden for loving me.

One rainy morning Angela found a sealed envelope with her name typed across the front sitting on her desk at work.

It hadn't been there earlier when she'd dropped off her briefcase but now here it was, looking somehow both sinister and bold. *Ms. Angela Martin,* someone had typed, like an accusation. She put her coffee cup down and held the envelope up to the light, trying to see a signature or a sentence, some sort of clue about what was inside.

She couldn't figure out who had put it there. At 9:30 in the morning everybody in the school was either in class or in the main office, except for the girls who'd gotten their teachers to let them out to go to the bathroom (which was officially against the rules but what are you supposed to do when an adolescent girl asks to go to the bathroom?).

Not that it was unusual for notes to appear on a teacher's desk or in her box in the lounge. Maryfield Academy was run on paper. That was the big thing Serena, the biology teacher who didn't shave her legs, had gotten all worked up about: the trees, the forests, all the natural stuff this pointless communication was destroying. She'd gotten a grant from the Parents' Association to supply recycling bins for each classroom. She was the kind of teacher the students loved.

Angela gave up and opened the envelope. It was one brief paragraph of unsigned text typed on blank white stationery.

> One of the English teachers touched my breast. I've reported it but the principal doesn't care. I feel so uncomfortable at school now. I hate coming here every day. I knew, as a responsible adult, this would concern you. Please help.

At that moment, the bell rang and Angela stuffed the letter into her pocket. Her students, twenty-three sophomores, pushed their way in the door. She was an English teacher. Today they were supposed to discuss the part of *The Catcher in the Rye* where Holden's teacher, Mr. Antolini, touches him while he's sleeping in the guest room. Angela was unmoved by the irony.

She wasn't moved by much lately. She'd been department chair until last year when she'd gotten ousted over some petty thing they'd drummed up just to clean house. Her replacement, a favorite of the new principal, now made sure Angela got the biggest classes filled with as many mouthy, troubled, slacker kids as she could find. Of course, Angela couldn't prove a thing, not that anybody would have cared even if she could.

And now, six months before her fortieth birthday, just as she was getting adjusted to being treated like crap, somebody at Maryfield, this Catholic high school for girls, was busy anonymously accusing an English teacher of sex abuse. And on top of that, Angela happened to be a lesbian. It was just her luck.

Earlier that morning, Helen Blalock, the principal, had buried all her cigarettes in the backyard under a wet pot of pink geraniums. It was her fifth attempt in the past year and a half to stop and she was hopeful about this new technique she'd read in the *Southwest Shaman Magazine* she'd found at the local New Age bookstore. You were supposed to give the cigarettes back to the earth and say a silent prayer to the smoke spirits to help you lose the desire for tobacco. You were supposed to chant, "I yearn to breathe free. I have the strength to be me. I am a part of all I see. No more, no less than this tree."

And then you were supposed to walk over to the nearest tree and hug it for as long as you could.

Helen had worked in Catholic schools all her life and now, at fifty-three, she hoped this would be her last job before she got to retire and paint full time. She'd been hired at Maryfield just the year before probably both because she was dating a man on the Board of Trustees and because she was tall. Like all tall women, people attributed to her power, wisdom, and vision. Thus she was supposed to be able to save the school which had fallen on hard times. Although she enjoyed a challenge, she knew her limitations and enjoyed her pleasures: shopping for clothes, painting large canvasses which satirized female foibles, and watching British exports on TV. Most of her career she'd taught art.

She'd already smoked three cigarettes by the time Angela came into her office carrying the anonymous letter like a dead fish.

"Don't worry about it," she said, lighting a fourth. "None of the students has come to me with a complaint. It'll blow over. Some kid is probably angry about a grade."

So Angela took the opportunity to mention that she'd heard Annie Klinestiver, a senior, was three months pregnant.

Helen groaned.

"It gets worse," Angela said. "The kids are saying it's from her brother."

"We'll put her in the back row. The robe will cover most of the evidence," Helen said. She was talking about graduation which was only a few months away. The school didn't need any more negative publicity.

Just then the fire alarm went off. Five short blasts and a long one, repeated for a full forty-five seconds. Five long and one short was for earthquake or was it the other way around?

Helen left her office to watch over the twenty neat rows of girls who had lined up on the central terrace. She stood at the top of the landing leading down to it so everybody could see her in her expensive tweed suit, Ferragamo pumps, still-blonde hair piled high on her head in a loose bun. She smiled warmly at the entire community, giving a special wave to the assistant principal, whom she disliked, shouting out instructions on a portable microphone.

The assistant principal, a short, plump nun, was dressed in a pale blue A-line skirt and white Peter Pan blouse. Already, even this early in the morning, she had circles of perspiration under her arms which everybody could see because of the way she was waving and gesturing to achieve order in the ranks. When that was done, she walked over to Helen and whispered in her ear. Helen suspected Rose James of secret drinking; her hot breath always smelled like sour grapes, but she couldn't do anything about it. The Dominicans owned the school and those women took care of their own.

"Did you schedule this?" Sister R. J. said. Since she herself was in charge of fire drills, discipline, and the academic schedule, and protected her purview like a nursing bitch, Helen was surprised.

"Of course not," she said. Rose James twitched and Helen fought an urge to pat her on the tightly permed brown head. "You didn't?"

"Must be a prank," she said, "or worse. I think we should call a faculty meeting. Tell all. Get it out into the open. Force the devil into the light of day."

"Oh, good God," Helen said. "I suppose you're right. I keep hoping it will just go away." She was still hoping so hard she'd let Angela believe hers was the first anonymous note anybody'd received. In fact, she'd gotten three before Angela's, all saying nearly the same thing.

"Fat chance," Rose James said, looking out over the lines of girls. "Somebody's gone mad."

Thirty years ago the school had been the gem of the order. On six acres of prime land, the old estate had been given to the church by a doctor whose wife had died there of tuberculosis. He'd tried to turn the place, an Italianate villa surrounded by orange groves and park-like grounds, into a sanitarium, but the city wouldn't allow it, so he willed it to the church instead. The nuns had built modern buildings on the northern edge of the land, leaving the villa intact to use as a location for film shoots and wedding receptions.

Which was extremely prescient of them given the fact that enrollment had been falling for ten years straight and one day's rental was nearly $1,000. Despite everybody's best efforts with recruiting and publicity, Maryfield seemed cursed. Too many girls' schools in the area, a declining birthrate, the neighboring boys' school going coed, everybody analyzed the cause differently. Some privately speculated that the student council president caught necking with her girlfriend in the school parking lot was the final kiss of death.

Helen had known the problems when she applied, but she'd only counted on normal crises when she took the job. Who could have imagined anything like this? There was something demonic about it; Rose James was right. Something possessed. Like the devil was sitting right on top of the bell tower pulling strings, laughing as he watched them all jump and flinch and twist in the wind.

After Sister Rose James left to oversee roll call, Helen looked out over the students in their gray pleated skirts, white blouses, and penny loafers. White/black, rich/poor, gifted and average, they were generally good kids who'd either lucked out and gotten decent parents or hadn't, in which case Maryfield or a place like it was the next best thing. Usually, even the screwups graduated and went to college.

Next, she watched the teachers standing at the head of each line of girls, taking roll: three men, all the rest women, most of them past forty. When she took the job only a couple of old-timers quit. Everybody else was either giving her a chance or was too lazy to move on, probably because the former principal was such a burnout case, Helen looked pretty good. She'd gotten rid of a few unproductive department chairs, fired the bookkeeper, and hired a campus minister. But overall, except for a few weirdos and a couple of smart-asses, nobody seemed headed for trouble. That's what made this thing such a mystery. She couldn't figure out what teacher or student would be bothered to stir up something crazy like this.

Angela had left Helen's office when the alarm went off and now she was standing at the head of her line, holding a large white sign over her head which read SCR-TAN, the first three letters of the kids' last names. She looked up at the principal watching all of them from the landing. Did Helen suspect that the anonymous note had been written about her? She was an English teacher after all. Maybe Helen was putting her on about not taking it seriously. Maybe she was suspicious as hell.

At least she'd taken the note right in when she got it. How many accused pedophiles would do that? When Sister Rose James blew her whistle Angela lowered her sign. She took a couple of deep breaths to get ahold of herself. As far as she knew, all anybody at Maryfield understood was that she wasn't married. And besides, just because she wasn't straight didn't mean she liked teenage girls.

The next day, the worst of the rains started. Nobody could remember when there'd been so much in so short a time. Although she'd resisted telling the faculty about the notes for weeks, Helen decided R. J. was probably right about getting it out in the open. But before she could call a faculty meeting, the terrace flooded and the janitors had to sandbag the thresholds of all the classrooms on the lower side of the school, which so severely taxed the older of the two that he'd had symptoms of a heart attack. Luckily, he'd only pulled a muscle near his breastbone but the noise from ambulances and squad cars had disrupted classwork to such an extent that several teachers gave up on their lesson plans and let their students watch the action from the windows.

After that, two students had a car accident on their way back from an off-campus lunch because of slippery roads and poor visibility. Helen feared a lawsuit even though their crashing into a street light had nothing to do with the school. Finally, when rain started pouring into the library through the roof, Helen canceled school for the rest of the week to repair the damage.

On their second day off all the teachers received this letter in the mail:

Dear Parents,
It has come to my attention that Sally Hamington, an English teacher at our school, is a pedophile. I regret to inform you of this, but in order to deal with such a pressing issue, I am calling on all of you to report any incidents of child molestation that have been perpetrated by this individual so we can press viable charges.
Yours sincerely, Helen Blalok

At home, Angela read the letter with delight. Well, maybe delight was too strong a word, but relief was too weak. The main thing was that it wasn't Angela who was being accused. The second was that the person they'd named instead was Sally Hamington. Sally Hamington was the replacement department chair who'd made Angela's life miserable. What she had secretly wished for, that Sally'd leave the school, might now be coming true. Or maybe they'd at least make her step down from being chair. To celebrate, Angela threw the whole set of uncorrected vocabulary quizzes she'd been working on into the trash and then did something she enjoyed. She wrote a sonnet, in perfect rhyming iambic pentameter, about the beauty of love and the shortness of life. She'd figure out what to tell her students had happened to the quizzes the next day.

After reading the same letter, several other teachers called Helen in a panic.

She made a mental note not to renew any of their contracts, even though decent teachers were hard to come by. Not only was the thing written on photocopied Maryfield letterhead, but her last name was misspelled. And what idiot would believe she would announce that Sally Hamington had been accused of pedophilia to the parents at large?

Helen toasted an onion bagel and slathered it with cream cheese. She needed something to chew on even though she knew she was gaining weight. All this stress was not good for her diet but there was no way to win when you had a job like hers. She should have stayed in her first job out of college as a graphic designer and waited for things to open up in the professional world instead of rushing into education like a scared rabbit. But it was obviously too late to think about that now.

After the bagel, she lit a cigarette and changed the channel from the rerun of Sherlock Holmes she'd been watching to *Unsolved Mysteries*. This segment had been partly filmed at the Maryfield villa and had earned the school $5,000. That thought made her feel a little better. And there he was, Robert Stack, wooden and vaguely cadaverous, standing in the Renaissance portico, announcing the subject of the next segment—the discovery in a European hilltown of the remains of six children, all of whom the residents had thought were away at boarding school somewhere else.

Don't let it be in Italy, Helen thought. People there are too civilized for murder. People there believe in food and sex and wine and art and bicycles. Wasn't any place civilized anymore?

The next Monday, the rains stopped. Several dozen waterlogged library books in the biological science, medieval society, and American fiction sections had been disposed of. Five classroom floors had been waxed by the custodians and faculty gossip circles had formed all over campus, hardly bothering to disperse when either students or administrators walked by.

"Teacher or student?" Serena said to Angela, by the coffee machine in the faculty lounge. They were waiting for Helen's postponed meeting to begin.

Serena was sipping a cup of dark tea that smelled like dirt. It had twigs and wormy things floating around on top.

"What are you drinking?" Angela said.

"Some herbal tea I blend myself. Do you have a problem with that?"

Too late Angela remembered that Serena was very touchy about her eco/homeopathic habits. And yet she flaunted them almost as if she wanted people to react. Hairy legs and she always wore skirts and sometimes stockings. Herbal tea with gross things floating in it. Still, she was the closest thing to a friend Angela had at work so she tried to overlook her crankiness.

"I have no idea," Angela said, changing the subject. "I'm just glad it didn't turn out to be about me."

"It could have been any of us," Serena said, looking at her funny.

"Well, yeah. I just mean if it was going to be about an English teacher, I'm glad it wasn't me."

"It's obviously untrue," Serena said.

"Well, of course," Angela said. She realized she needed to slow down and think about what she was going to say before she said it. Did she sound too unsympathetic to Sally?

It was true that the validity of the accusation was never in question. The accuser couldn't have chosen a less likely person to call a pedophile than creepy Sally Hamington. Angela couldn't imagine her shaking hands with the principal much less touching a kid's breast. It was like she kept a glass wall between herself and the rest of the world.

"Poor Sally," Angela said. "Such a great teacher, so demanding. Such an asset to the school. This must be terribly upsetting to her." She knew she didn't lie well. Her face was so hot she worried that Serena might notice the flush.

"Something wrong?" she said.

"No," Angela said. "Except that all this is so weird. It's like an earthquake, coming out of nowhere, shaking things up."

She hated Sally Hamington because, aside from stacking her classes with losers, she was always finding fault with Angela's work, her lesson plans, her grading policy, her classroom management. Sally had a poker up her ass and the thing was that Helen liked her, so Angela had to live in fear that she'd get hauled on the carpet or even fired for some dumb thing.

Angela had actually been Sally's department chair for awhile. That hadn't been much better than this. Sally criticized her work then, too, and went behind her back to the principal, but Angela wasn't afraid of her like now. Now Sally had power.

The story Angela had heard when she'd done a background check on Sally for the job at Maryfield five years ago was that she'd tried to be a police officer but she'd failed the interview by saying she'd give a speeding ticket even if the recipient was a close relative. This was taken as evidence that she was lacking in the human touch which was a big deal after the Rodney King incident.

Great. So she becomes a high school English teacher. Not like she cared about the beauty of the language, the wisdom of the writers, or her students' creativity at all. Vocabulary, grammar, footnotes, the ten characteristics of Anglo-Saxon poetry, the exact number of times nature is referred to in *Frankenstein,* the type of meter in a Shakespearean sonnet.

In the old days, before the former principal burned out and got bitter about struggling with enrollment, Angela remembered that teachers were valued for their love of the subject, their insight and wit. Now, people like Sally Hamington were rewarded for the number of tests they gave. Instead of having discussions in the faculty lounge about art and music and the latest *New Yorker,* people bitched about how dumb the kids were and how every year they got lazier than the year before.

Sally wanted to be known as the toughest teacher at Maryfield. She produced pages and pages of charts, syllabi, policy objectives, all in tiny type reduced on the Xerox machine. Her kids failed by the dozens, missing the passing grade by .001 of a point. She smirked when somebody mentioned how afraid they were of her. No wonder somebody wanted to ruin her life. Angela understood the motivation perfectly.

It was time for the faculty meeting to begin. She and Serena went to sit down, but not next to each other. Angela wanted to be in the back of the room, where nobody could see the expression on her face.

Helen walked in with two men and a woman and formally introduced them to everybody there. One of the men was white, about thirty-five, with a thin brown moustache across his upper lip: Chuck Grossman, private eye. The other one was black, about fifty, plump and jovial. He was Jerome Brooks, forensic psychologist. The woman was the school lawyer, an alumna on the Board of Trustees named Theresa de Cervantes. What Angela noticed first about them as they sat down in a line across the front of the room was how hard they were all smiling. It was unnerving as hell.

Sally sat in a chair off by herself, expressionless, staring straight ahead. Angela snuck a long look at her crisply pressed skirt and blouse, short hair, symmetrical features. Everything was totally utilitarian as usual, even her face.

Chuck Grossman was explaining how the group had been hired by the school to look into the matter of anonymous notes accusing Sally Hamington of pedophilia.

He leaned forward in his chair as if he wanted to make serious eye contact with each of them. "We've gotten some fine fingerprints off a couple of the letters sent to faculty homes," he said. "The circle of suspicion is getting smaller, closing in."

This was evidently Helen's cue to go to the blackboard and outline the chronology and substance of the harassment, which had begun weeks before with a couple of notes to her naming a member of the English department, a similar one to several faculty members, and finally the letter to everybody in the room purportedly asking parents to offer evidence. She'd kept everything quiet to protect Sally until the writer had gone public with the last note.

She misspelled the word "anonymous" but nobody said anything. Angela smiled to think how it must have been driving Sally crazy not to correct her.

"Obviously," Dr. Brooks interrupted Helen to say, "there is no substance to any of the allegations." He wiped his forehead with a handkerchief. Everybody nodded and looked warmly at Sally who continued to stare at a place near the coffee maker. He was right. It was impossible.

Helen sat back down next to him and continued. "Sally has been a brick through all of this and has been helping in the investigation in every way possible."

Angela noticed that Helen had never once looked at Sally the entire time, which was encouraging. Maybe Sally was losing favorite teacher status, being the center of such an embarrassing and time-consuming scandal. Maybe Angela's dreams would come true.

"We need you to refrain from talking to one another and speculating about all of this," Helen continued. "We need to continue to work as normally as possible."

Yeah, right, Angela thought to herself. She'd probably told half a dozen people here how miserable Sally had made her life over the years. She inched behind Gabe, the big Spanish teacher, and tried not to look guilty. She tried to look like everybody else, concerned, surprised, even angry that such an injustice should be disrupting their lives.

Helen reached up to write the psychologist's office number on the board for anybody who was upset by the difficult atmosphere, which was probably a code way to describe the perpetrator.

Suddenly somebody near Angela spoke.

"I'm feeling so uncomfortable." It was Jennifer, an economics teacher. "It's like you think one of us is doing it."

Lots of big, noncommittal, benign smiles from the panel. Finally the lawyer said, "We want to support you. We're here to solve this."

Helen nodded.

Sally began to tear at a cuticle.

"We're doing all we can," Helen said. "We will catch this deeply troubled person."

"It's somebody who knows the school very well," Chuck, the detective said. "It's somebody who knows teachers' habits and addresses."

"The suspect is unbalanced, teetering on the brink," the psychologist said. "For some reason this person has fixated on Sally. Undoubtedly they are enjoying all the distress they are causing. They are weak, too insecure to deal with anger directly. Thus the accusations, the secrecy. Unwittingly Sally might remind them of something unresolved in their past."

"If any of you suspect anything or anyone, please come to me or to Sister Rose James as soon as possible," Helen said. "I'll leave Dr. Brooks's number on the board."

Jennifer began to weep. Sally looked at her with disdain.

"We're sitting here suspecting one another. It's sick. I feel like I'm going to explode."

Good old primary process Jennifer. Angela wished she'd thought of that. Nobody would ever suspect somebody who broke down under the emotional pressure of the meeting. The real culprit would act just like her, hiding behind somebody's back.

That night Helen Blalock masturbated for two hours before finally falling asleep. By that time her hand was numb and useless. She'd never had an orgasm in her life. She'd get to the edge of one and then her mind would turn on and she'd lose the direction, everything would dissolve, and she'd lie there wanting to wring somebody's neck.

She dreamed about Sally, the oddball who'd caused all hell to break loose. She used to like her, admire her even, her tall lean body, her focus, her output, her complete confidence in the correctness of her point of view, her impatience with anybody who was lazy or without self-control. Helen had made her English department chair for exactly that reason, to clean up systems and demand better work.

Now she found all that annoying. For the good of the school, why couldn't she just quit? Was the ultimate justice Sally Hamington sought worth all Helen had done to promote positive publicity for Maryfield? She'd even gotten the lawyer to hint, before going public to the faculty, about a year's salary, health benefits, and generous letters of recommendation.

In return, Sally had suggested that nobody was doing enough to catch the perp. The hidden cameras they'd installed a couple of weeks before in her classroom were at the wrong angle; the faculty room, where several of the notes had been left, didn't even have one. The investigators were idiots; Helen wasn't pushing them hard enough. Sally wanted to run the show; she made it clear. She always thought she could do things better than anyone else.

In Helen's dream, Sally fell off a huge cliff and Helen caught her right before she hit the ground. Just the way she always caught herself before she had an orgasm.

A week or so later, Helen, Sister Rose James, and Chuck Grossman, P.I., were sitting in Helen's office watching films taken by the camera hidden in Sally's classroom. They fast-forwarded through normal activities and long dark nights until one Tuesday morning at 2 a.m. when the lights sprang on.

"Look," Chuck said. Thank God there was finally something to look at. This case was driving him nuts; all the innuendo, the ugly petty gossip and grudges that develop in a small community. It reminded him of that play he'd read in high school, *The Crucible,* where everybody pointed the finger at everybody else and where, just like here, they were all supposed to be these super good Christians.

He was so irritable that he'd spent the last half hour while they ran the video baiting poor Sister Rose James, just for the hell of it.

"You want her out of the way," he'd said. "You want her job, don't you?"

"Don't be ridiculous," the nun said. "No one envies the life of a classroom teacher—correcting papers, planning lessons. I did that already, for twenty-five years."

One thing about this job is that it had chewed up all his preconceptions about self-denying nuns and schoolteachers. And any good detective knows that preconceptions never help an investigation. He'd heard enough stories about baby-faced killers, cashmere-coated shoplifters, and crazy psychiatrists to be certain of that.

"Wow," he said now. "Look at that."

They watched the screen as a disembodied arm reached across the desk and deposited a piece of paper on it.

"Slow it down," Helen said. "Rewind and slow it down."

"Sally's hand," R. J. said.

"How can you tell?" Chuck said. "The ring? Nails?"

"Why on earth would it be her hand?" Helen said, lighting a cigarette. It was her office and she could smoke if she wanted to. She'd never be able to stop until this thing was over, she might as well admit it and if she did, she'd start putting on weight even faster than she was now.

Last week at the faculty meeting everybody had seemed to admire her composure and discretion in the face of such a bizarre situation. But now, against her explicit injunction, people were whispering about the case and the music teacher, Linda Samuels of all people, had risen up as a vocal critic of her methods and lack of decisiveness in the face of all the detective bumbling. At Sally's prompting, Helen guessed. And worst of all, a few veteran teachers were starting to bring up the old principal's name, as in "She would have handled this much better than Blalock."

"If it is her hand, why is she trying to avoid the camera?" Chuck said. "She knows it's focused on her desk. What's she doing here at 2 a.m. putting something on her own desk?"

"Unless. . . " R. J. said.

"What?" he said.

"Ah," Helen said. The light. "She could be doing it to herself." The detective looked at her. Her face was hidden behind a cloud of cigarette smoke so thick he couldn't read her expression.

"Funny," he said. "That's what she said about you."

"Sally?" Helen said.

"That you could be the perpetrator. That you never liked her. That you're threatened by tall, strong women who hold the line against mediocrity and sloth." He'd chosen the word "sloth" deliberately to add religious weight to the accusation. Of course Sally had never said such a thing. But it wasn't a lie exactly. She had told Chuck she thought Helen was a stupid fool. Besides, it was his job to jerk everybody around and see what took.

"She thinks you're the one?" R. J. said. She looked back at the screen, where the hand was caught on pause. "It could just as well be yours, I guess. You're both big. Big fingers, flat at the tips, ring on the fourth."

Helen laughed. "Don't be silly. Chuck's making it up to get a reaction." She jabbed him on the arm. She liked to flirt a little bit, especially in the afternoon. She hadn't had a man for a couple of years, since she'd made the mistake of going to bed with that married banker on the Board of Trustees.

Chuck fast forwarded, two hours, three days, a week. They stared, hypnotized, at the classroom scenes picked up by the camera: girls writing in their notebooks, listening to Sally, bursts of laughter, more writing, hands raised, somebody falling asleep. Dark nights, empty desks and then, during a free period, Sally's form slinking along the blackboard toward her desk.

"What the heck is she doing?" Rose James said.

"Trying to stay out of camera angle," the detective said. "But why?"

"She's playing with us," Helen said. "Checking to see if we're actually reviewing the tapes."

Nobody said anything.

"Well that would be in character, wouldn't it? She'd be delighted to point out our ineptitude, wouldn't she? Blame us for the whole thing instead of the mysterious perpetrator."

"You have to call her in, don't you? To find out what she's doing?" Rose James said to Chuck.

"I think we should wait," he said. Technically, Helen and R. J. were suspects, not coinvestigators, but he'd found that cozying up to those in charge of a place usually smoothed out his job.

"What I want to know is why she would be doing it to herself?" Helen said. "It still doesn't make any sense."

"That's the point," Rose James said. "If she was doing it to herself it's because she's insane."

"Or," Chuck said.

"Or what?" Helen said.

"Or she's trying to screw up the school because she wants to get you fired."

"Why would she want to get her fired?" R. J. said.

"Maybe she thinks she'd be a better principal, too."

Helen's heart began to race. This was going to be her last job, goddamn it. No Sally Hamington was going to screw things up.

After they left, Helen held her head in her hands. She pressed her fingers into her temples. She had the beginnings of a killer headache and she had a Parents' Association dinner tonight for which she needed to be in top condition in case they'd heard anything about the anonymous notes and tried to nail her with tough questions. Some of them did that, particularly the men, the short men with high-achieving wives. They liked to try to trip her up about policies and statistics, just for the fun of it.

And Rose James was no help. In fact, sometimes Helen got a little paranoid about her, like maybe she enjoyed seeing Helen squirm. She never jumped in to help her out, that was for sure. What if she was involved in the Sally thing? Chuck obviously found the idea within the realm of possibility.

What if she had a secret crush on Sally and had been rebuffed and was taking out her rage in this sick, cloistered, claustrophobic way? Or else was Rose James herself the pedophile and accusing somebody else put everybody off her track? Certainly there were plenty of priests who had touched little boys. Why not nuns and girls?

Helen shook her head. That was crazy. This whole investigation was making her crazy. She thought of the dimpled, permed nun. Poor thing. Soft and spongy like the Pillsbury Doughboy. Helen's headache began to lift. A silly thought crossed her mind. Did Rose James masturbate? If she did, Helen hoped R. J. was luckier than she was.

Sally sat on a bench overlooking the central terrace where the students lined up for fire drills, ate lunch, and had outdoor assemblies. Seniors had staked out the wide expanse of stairs leading to the raised area where speakers stood and skits were performed. The Senior Steps were their privilege, that and leaving campus every day for a lunch of greasy, overpriced fast food from which they returned lethargic and late and sometimes stoned.

But Sister R. J. insisted on ensuring them this right even when the girls abused it day after day. Sally suspected that she was in the pocket of the local pizza parlor, chicken drive-through, and beef bowl establishments. The burger joints were popular enough already.

Sally was glad she didn't teach seniors. They were too hard to intimidate; most of them didn't give a damn about their grades and the Advanced Placement kids all thought they were smarter than the teachers anyway. And you couldn't deny that affirmative action had screwed up the Mexicans because they got into college no matter what. Only the Asians were still OK although they were so quiet in class they might as well not have been in the room at all.

She glanced at her classroom door across the yard. She didn't know exactly what she expected to see, maybe somebody going in with another anonymous note. Sheila Campbell maybe, the red-headed junior with fat thighs and no eyebrows. And the biggest mouth on campus. A couple of months ago, when Sheila turned in her term paper a day late on the intersection between Charlotte Brontë's personal life and *Jane Eyre* and Sally hadn't accepted it for credit, little Sheila had called in all the big guns. It was almost like she had set up the situation to see who would win.

There they had sat in Rose James's sterile office facing the mournful crucifix next to the awful needlepoint kitten on the wall behind her desk: the father, a top IRS manager; the mother, a bank officer; the sister, an alumna who was home for spring break from Stanford. And Sister Rose James, who didn't believe in holding the line on anything in the area of academics. She did seem to be obsessed with one part of her job: uniform regulations. Blouses had to be tucked in; the distance above the knee of pleated skirts was actually measured; she compared the shade of navy socks the kids wore to a standard sample. Sally figured it was probably a nun thing, her focus on the body. Everybody laughed at her behind her back.

So there they were, Sheila's entire pale, red-headed family, Rose James, and Sally, three days after the term paper deadline with no one, not even Rose James, sharing Sally's point of view, which was stated clearly in black and white on several official sheets of paper every student had in her possession, highlighted in yellow and signed by student, Sally, and guardian. Sally had brought facsimiles of these classroom regulations, put them in the middle of the table and said hardly a word during the entire meeting.

"The rules are clear," she had kept repeating.

Sheila rolled her eyes.

"Sheila was ill," her father said.

At which point Sally had read out loud the section about unforeseen absence.

The sister from Stanford sneered. She was in the middle of an Intro to Psychology class. She knew an anal retentive when she saw one.

Sheila had wept, her pink face getting red and blotchy, her teeny hands like an otter's working a piece of Kleenex into a ball and then a rope and finally tearing the whole thing apart and dropping it piece by piece onto the floor. Once, when nobody was watching, she had looked at Sally with such quick and secret rage it took her breath away. Her eyes were exactly like Charles Manson at his craziest, before the trial, before they cut his hair in prison, before all his girls carved up their foreheads, scarring themselves forever even after they renounced him and grew out their bangs.

Sister R. J. had ended up supporting Sally, but in an indirect and backhanded way so that Sally still felt betrayed and Sheila's parents actually winked at the nun on their way out the door. Sally let it go. She suspected that R. J. would change the kid's grade later in the computer behind her back.

Now, she stood up and headed for the girls' bathroom which she usually did three or four times during her lunch surveillance duty. Some teachers never even did it once, which was another reason why so many kids came to class loaded after lunch. Teachers pretended exaggerated behavior was caused by the high sugar content of the cafeteria food. Sally couldn't believe the way some people kidded themselves.

She banged the door open fast hoping to surprise somebody before they could pop their joint or cigarette into the john. Instead of that, what she found was Alice Todesco busily cutting a piece of flesh the size of a dime out of the palm of her hand.

"Alice, Alice, don't do that," Sally said half-heartedly. Alice was always making these public gestures to get attention or whatever the point was. The room was gray and dismal and smelled like a combination of urine, air freshener, and cigarettes. Strangely, Helen had tried to make it more appealing by getting the art club to paint perky zoo animals on the front of the stalls.

"What?" Alice said. Her eyes were totally flat, like she was just waking up.

"Why are you cutting yourself?" Sally hated this part of her job, this psychological, interpersonal garbage, but if it got the kid back into class it was probably worth the trouble.

"To let it out," Alice answered through half-open lids. She was leaning against one of the sinks.

"If you cut your hand you won't be able to take your test on *Julius Caesar* next period," Sally said. "You'll get blood all over the paper and I won't be able to read it. Come on outside with me, Alice. Be strong. Remember how Caesar said, 'Cowards die many times before their deaths; The valiant never taste of death but once.' There's just enough time to review before the bell rings."

"You're not going to tell Sister Rose James?" she said.

"Are you disappointed?"

Alice bent her head. Sally knew she didn't have to be so sarcastic but she caught Alice at this stuff every few weeks and the truth was that this self-pity made her sick. Her parents were probably too afraid of her to set proper limits.

"I can't help it," Alice said.

"So maybe a professional should be called in."

"I've been seeing David for five years now," Alice said. "We're working on impulse control."

The bell rang. Life went on. Sally told Alice to get a Band-Aid from the office and then she went into each empty stall to check for vandalism and contraband. Inside the door of stall number three she found another anonymous accusation about her. She sat down on the toilet and stared at it. It was worse than the rest. She felt her jaw tighten and salty saliva fill her mouth.

This is what she read:

Sally Hamington helps me after school.

She puts her arms around me and tells me she's a fool

for love. That age doesn't matter. That I'm no child.

She takes my nipple into her mouth; it drives her wild.

After she bites it she corrects my grammar.

I want to hit her over the head with a hammer.

Instead of throwing up, Sally hit her fist very hard against the graffiti. The door swung open and crashed against the front of the stall next to it. Then she licked two fingers and tried to rub the words off but they had evidently been written in indelible black felt pen. The second bell rang.

One thing was for sure. If it was a student, it had to be one of hers who had written it. Nobody else would have thought to use a semicolon correctly.

Rose James drove herself home at about 5:30. She had a beige '92 Taurus that she kept in good shape with the help of a mechanic in the parish who tuned it for free. She had a regular routine that she enjoyed, depended on, so much so that she rarely went out in the evening. If there was a teachers' party or an order event she went, of course, but she never ate and never drank anything except sparkling water. She tried to make such a strong impression with vibrant chatter that people remembered her having been there much longer than she actually stayed.

So by 8 p.m. at the latest, she'd excuse herself to use the ladies' room and never return. She'd sometimes even leave her headlights off until she was out of view of the gathering place and knew she had safely gotten away.

Her idiosyncrasies were nothing compared to some nuns she knew. One spent every lunch period gossiping with her students about their boyfriends and their families. Another one curried favor with wealthy parishioners in order to get beautiful gifts, use of their vacation homes, and actual cash on holy days, birthdays, and saint's days. Some were homosexual, but that was mostly a thing of the past. Most of those had left the order. Mostly everybody had.

So why did she stay?

Because she was homely, because she was scared. She knew she was the only kind of woman religious orders attracted anymore, the ones with nothing else but God. And lately, R. J. didn't really have God even, not the way she used to when she'd talked to Him like a father and like a lover, like somebody who loved a part of you nobody else even knew was there.

What she did have was her cat, Prissy, who slept curled around her head. Because R. J. lived in fear of losing her, too, Prissy never left the apartment except on a leash and R. J. prepared all her food from scratch. An entire shelf of her three-foot-long bookcase was devoted to cat books and they weren't just for decoration. She referred to them frequently: holistic cat health, baking for your kitty, courageous cat stories, every murder mystery with the word "cat" in the title, children's cat books, celebrities' cats, cat jokes she'd collected and mounted in a three-ring binder.

She lived for that cat she had to admit, but at least she came by it honestly. Her Irish great-grandmother was rumored to have owned twenty- five cats at a time in her peat cottage in County Cork. Her grandmother bred Maine coons for grocery money. She'd heard a story of some relative who kept a tomcat imprisoned in a cage in the kitchen and force-fed it Gerber's pureed liver three times a day. R. J. would never sink that far. She respected Prissy's feral feline nature. She gave the cat space, except for the leash of course. She only wished people would do the same for her.

What she did every night, both the nights with meetings or social events and the evenings when she had no responsibilities except to cook for Prissy and play catnip ball with her when she was done, was pour herself a glass of Christian Brothers wine (two was her limit what with so much alcoholism in the family), eat a frozen pizza or chicken pie or lasagna or burrito (why bother to cook when there were so many tasty things in the frozen food section they'd never allowed her to have in the convent?), and turn on her short-wave radio and listen to police calls or depending on her mood, local phone conversations, which was illegal but who was going to catch her?

There were also spin-offs of these interests: true crime paperbacks and police crime gazettes which were mostly bought by sickos who got excited by the graphic photos of bloody victims. But that wasn't her. It didn't turn her on to see the photos or read the reports. In fact she had to steel herself, force herself to look, but it was worth it, because of how she felt afterward.

She'd put her feet up on the ottoman, Prissy purring on her lap, take a sip of wine and think about her teeny-tiny life: nun, Dean of Discipline, one bedroom cinder block apartment, voyeuristic evenings, lonely weekends and feel so happy, so fulfilled, because none of the horrible things she heard or saw would ever happen to her.

Except that this Sally thing was beginning to grate on her. She figured she'd have to do something about it pretty soon. She was Dean of Discipline after all. Good luck getting another decent job in the archdiocese with anonymous accusations of pedophilia flying around Maryfield. Good luck depending on private detectives to solve the crime. In no way could she afford to jeopardize this life she'd made for herself. If she did, they'd send her to the Mother House which meant she might as well be dead.

The first thing Helen saw when she got to work the next morning was something black hanging from the flagpole. Her hand went to her throat. Was it the effigy of a nun? She got closer. No, it was a black garbage bag hanging halfway up the pole. Apparently there was something in it; that was the point, not what it looked like from a distance. She was certain it was another Sally Hamington incident but was surprised that the perpetrator had been this bold.

She lowered the bag slowly. The object in it wasn't very heavy, maybe eight or ten pounds, but it was ungainly; it kept flopping from side to side. Helen stopped to get her breath. She felt watched. She wanted to turn around fast and catch somebody peeping around a corner or from the bushes. She wanted to turn around and scream, "Alright, you son of a bitch. Leave us alone. You sick jerk." But she didn't. She played her part like a well-paid actor or a puppet. The whole thing was beginning to get very scary.

She tried to imagine the person doing this. It had to have been done in the dark with a flashlight, equipment, bag, rope. She sometimes felt that if she could picture the action, if she was able to picture the face, like those psychics you see on TV helping stumped police departments find who threw the mutilated body into the woods, she could solve the case.

Helen put the bag onto the ground. She had a bad feeling they'd never solve this damn thing and then everybody would blame her. They'd say she'd handled the situation ineptly. As if it had anything to do with her. Blame the principal when anything hit a snag. Some teacher quits abruptly, they blame her. A kid gets caught doing drugs in the john, blame Helen. Not enough endowment, enrollment, scholarships to Ivy League schools, blame her, blame her, blame her.

The bag moved and there was a muffled whine. Quickly she untied the knot at the top and looked inside. A squirming black puppy jumped into her arms. She put it on the ground. It was wet and smelled like urine. She'd never been an animal lover. The parakeets she kept in a cage at home were enough for her.

But the dog kept whimpering and clawing at her legs to get picked up. So instead of letting it rip her stockings to shreds, she bent over and patted it on the head.

"Yes, yes," she said. Then she saw the inevitable note attached to its collar.

> Return me to Sally Hamington. She'll have missed me by now. One minute I'm sleeping next to her bed. The next minute she's terrified I'm dead.

Helen sat down on the cold cement bench near the flagpole and let the puppy lick her face. This must be Blackie, the dog Sally and her husband Walt had trained to fetch the newspaper before it could lift much more than the metro section in its mouth. She knew she should get up and take the dog into her office where nobody would see it but somehow she couldn't seem to move. What she really wanted to do was put her face in Blackie's stinky fur and have a good long cry.

When Sally arrived at work she knocked at Helen's door and then walked in. Blackie was sitting in Helen's lap, chewing the top of one of her pencils.

"You shouldn't let her do that," Sally said. "It's not good for her to ingest lead."

"Aren't you upset?" Helen said. "Somebody went to your house and stole your dog. Somebody has begun to include your family in the intimidation. Who knows where it will end?"

"I don't want her chewing on that pencil."

"She's mouthing the eraser," Helen said with great fatigue. Sally was so annoying. She ought to be apologizing for causing so much stress and confusion instead of lecturing her on pet care. At least she ought to be acting like a human being and expressing some concern.

"Listen, it's none of my business; she's your dog, but I think she was weaned too early," Helen said. "I've been holding her like this for half an hour."

"It's called teething," Sally said. "It's normal. Besides she's been traumatized."

Helen thought she saw Sally's eyes well up with tears. Finally.

"Of course nobody saw anything," Sally said like an accusation after regaining her composure. Then she strode over to take Blackie away. Helen flinched slightly. She had an impulse to hang on as if the dog were hers. Poor thing. How would you like to be Sally Hamington's dog? Helen kissed Blackie on the top of her head and handed her over.

"I'll need a couple of subs while I take her home," she said.

After Sally and the dog left her office, Helen tried her damnedest to remember if Sally had acted suspicious. Rose James had suggested that maybe Sally was doing this stuff to herself. Had she tied up her own dog and sent her up the flagpole? And if she had, why? Helen couldn't fathom it. The explanation couldn't involve her. Besides, it didn't need to. She'd changed her mind. There were probably a dozen people on campus who would have gladly tried to get rid of her if they thought they could get away with it.

She thought about Sally going to her home with the dog. She imagined several small rooms in a boxy tract house, lots of cement outside, a tiny patch of grass, all the rooms turned into offices and work spaces for her school work and the video editing company she and her husband were starting up. One bed, one couch, spotless kitchen, white bathroom, family photos and heirlooms on a table in the living room. Maybe a china tea cup and saucer decorated with tiny roses, maybe a brass baby shoe and a lacquered trinket from Chinatown. The last thing the house would be was sensuous or aesthetically pleasing.

"Do you want protection?" Helen had asked her. She was torn. If the police got involved it was only a matter of time before parents and students found out. But how were they going to solve anything with only one P.I. on the job? "After all they did come into your home to take the dog. Even if they didn't hurt her. The point is the thing has

escalated almost to the point of violence. To the point of police in-
volvement."

"No," Sally'd snapped. "No police. It'll get out to the newspaper.
Everybody always believes the allegation when it comes to sexual assault, especially with kids."

"I wonder why that is?" Helen mused.

Sally looked at her sharply.

"I mean," she said, "if what you're saying is true. Which it may not
be. Especially in your case. Nobody in their right mind could imagine
you doing what those anonymous notes are suggesting. Nobody in
the world."

Angela got to work early because of a couple of lucky breaks at
Starbucks; a parking place had opened up right in front of the store
and for some reason there wasn't anybody in line.

"Wow," she said to the clerk. "Café latte, low-fat milk. Nobody
else here. Wow! This has never happened to me before."

The coffee guy could have cared less.

"Uh huh," he said.

Then, immediately, the line got long. It had been a slight lull, not a
miracle, for God's sake. Angela felt like a dope.

At work, the first thing she saw was Sally Hamington going into
the principal's office, probably about some new anonymous incident.
She felt a strange sensation come to her chest. She was actually jealous
that Sally was getting so much attention. Everybody in the administration was probably terribly concerned about her and right now they
were all sitting close together and reading over the new note and speculating about who had written it.

A few minutes later, on her way to the lounge with her Starbuck's
cup, Angela noticed Sally come out Helen's door with something in
her arms. Had she been given a gift? Angela walked closer and tried
to see. Sally was bending her head over it like she was cooing to an in-
fant. What could it be?

"It's my dog," Sally said. "I see you, Angela, watching me."

Angela jumped, dropping half the coffee onto her skirt.

"Shit," she said.

"You're here early," Sally said. For once, she meant. She was so like that, always subtly suggesting that you were doing something wrong. Angela knew for a fact that she'd labeled her as both lazy and polemical, interested in advancing her own left-wing political agenda in the classroom to the detriment of important skills like grammar and topic sentences.

Or maybe she was accusing Angela of something with the dog.

"What's happened to the dog?" she asked innocently. But too late she realized she shouldn't have asked it that way, that maybe it suggested some foreknowledge she shouldn't have. "I mean why's it here?"

"Somebody ran her up the flagpole with a threatening note tied to her collar. I'm not supposed to discuss it."

"Wow," Angela said. "She OK?"

"Yeah. I wish she could talk or at least point."

"Why?"

"So she could tell me who did it, obviously," Sally said. And then she put Blackie down onto the ground. Without hesitation the dog ran up to Angela and pissed all over her right foot.

"Swell," Angela said. She pushed the dog away from her. "What's she doing that for?"

"She's upset," Sally said. "Don't push her."

"She pissed on my foot." God, she couldn't believe it. Coffee on her skirt; dog pee on her foot.

"So take off your shoe and wash your foot," Sally said, leashing Blackie. Then she turned and walked away, snapping the dog to attention beside her heel.

Sally didn't come back for the rest of the day. Over the phone Helen Blalock told her to take the week off, on advice of the school lawyer, Theresa de Cervantes. Sally refused. One day was enough. She lived forty-five minutes away so it was too far to come back today after delivering the dog, but two days were unnecessary. For what? To give the perpetrator the satisfaction of forcing her out, of winning?

To rest, Helen had told her. Because of all the recent stress. To protect the dog from further harm.

To think about resigning, Sally said. Wasn't that what she was getting at? I thought I was the victim.

No, No. For your protection and peace of mind.

And at that Sally hung up and slammed her fist on the kitchen table, sloshing half the beer she'd poured for herself all over the table. After she wiped it up, she took out her lesson plans, grade book, three sets of essays, two textbooks, and began to work.

Back at Maryfield, her students were aware that something was wrong. Especially the juniors. In their three years of English classes including summer school, half of which had been taught by Sally, never once had she been out. Never once before today had they had a reprieve from constant terror and total accountability for every word of the night's thirty-page reading assignment or endless vocabulary lists or forty-page term papers or whatever the deal was that day. And, you couldn't feel like crap yourself for any reason: cramps, too much meth, your best friend's suicide attempt, or just because you decided to watch TV or pluck your eyebrows or talk on the phone too long. Behave like a teenager? No way. She had a second sense about when you hadn't done your work, when you were trying to hide behind somebody, or copy their homework.

Hamington was never out even when she was too sick to talk or stand up. She must have had no life except they knew she had a husband because they'd seen the prematurely bald man at the league basketball game she'd kept score for. They had watched her rub his arm during half time. Nobody could believe it. It caused them to have to imagine her having sex which made them shudder. She probably tied him up or handcuffed him to the headboard or spanked him, somebody who knew about these things suggested.

But today when the idiot religion teacher walked in to sub, they were almost disappointed. They were almost traumatized. It was like a loss of innocence. Sure they complained but it was a lot better having Ms. Hamington to always hold them accountable, to always be a bitch, to always be there.

The closest they came to expressing any of this was when Alice Todesco said in a quavering voice, "Where's Ms. Hamington?"

And the religion teacher, Rick Barnhardt, who would have told all the dirt had he known any, simply said. "I dunno. I do what they tell me. I just work here."

And there wasn't even an assignment for them to do.

"You're kidding," they said.

"No," he said. And then, well aware that he had absolutely no capacity to command respect, he yelled, "So shut up and find some other homework to do."

And, to his surprise, they did. In fact they figured out what Ms. Hamington would have assigned if she'd had time and then they did it. Mr. Barnhardt took it as evidence of new pedagogical authority and command and from that day forward actually showed some improvement in classroom management skills.

It was 3:30 the next morning and Angela was just finishing a full-fledged nightmare about Sally Hamington. Somebody else might have experienced it as a pleasant diversion, an agreeable vignette, but when Angela woke up, all twisted in her sheet and sweaty, she wanted to spit. The dream, there was no denying it, was a colorful sex film with her and Sally as the erotic stars. And what made it worse than that even, what made it a true nightmare, was that in the dream she'd really wanted Sally, begged her for deep kisses and full penetration and everything else she could think of.

She got up even though it was still dark out, and turned on the television to try to forget the awful pictures in her head. But, of course, the dream was etched in her memory forever, she who usually couldn't remember her dreams at all.

One thing was for sure. The Sally Hamington affair was working on her in ugly ways, stirring up things in her unconscious she didn't even know were there.

Helen Blalock called the faculty together again after school. It had been particularly windy and people were on edge. Every period a student or two was sent to the office because of misbehavior. One girl was accused of sneering at a teacher, another of having unclean thoughts.

In senior religion classes the students were in the middle of a teen parenting simulation where they were required to carry ten-pound bags of flour around for two weeks to see how it felt. Most of the girls had made baby clothes for the bags and carried them in harnesses like real infants, hardly leaving them alone for a minute. But today there was a rash of kidnappings for ransom and students had to pay big bucks. If they lost their baby they flunked the class, which meant not only no diploma but no grad night or prom.

On top of all that, something was wrong with the refrigeration in the cafeteria. Everybody who ate a hamburger got sick after lunch so that everybody else who went into the bathroom had to gag from the evil smell and sometimes got sick, too.

By the time she convened the meeting with a prayer, Helen Blalock hadn't been to the bathroom in six hours. She simply hadn't had time. And to make matters worse, recently she'd started to leak every time she coughed, a side effect of menopause, the gynecologist had told her.

Today she'd already smoked half a pack of cigarettes and eaten an entire box of greasy french fries she'd ordered from a kid going off-campus for lunch. She'd never sunk this low before, ordering take-out from a student. It was almost as bad as teachers buying marijuana from student suppliers, which she'd heard happened on public high school campuses sometimes. But she was too stressed to care.

Now, in the school library where, in spite of the smell of mildew from the recent rains, the faculty was gathering, she entreated the four corners of the earth in traditional Navajo fashion. She'd traveled to Santa Fe at Christmas and visited a sweat lodge and a shaman. At the hotel gift shop she'd found a poster that gave this prayer:

> *East*—To the source of inspiration, home of the powers of intelligence, give us clarity of thought and dedication to truth.
> *South*—To the source of passion, home of fire and spirit, give us the courage of commitment to the causes we believe in.
> *West*—To the source of emotion, home of the waters of caring and connection to each other, grant us the ability to give and receive love freely.
> *North*—To the source of power, home of the great earth mother, giver of all life and ground of our being, help us be aware of our rootedness in you.

Today she recited it to the group complete with arm and hand gestures provided by the dance teacher stationed to one side of her. A few people giggled but she didn't care. Barbarians and Visigoths, Huns and bourgeoisie. One of the religion teachers scowled at her, wanting some traditional Catholic prayer, like a Hail Mary, probably. Nobody in the room except for Helen and the French teacher traveled at all.

"Yesterday," she began, "Sally's dog, Blackie, was stolen from her yard and strung up the flagpole in a heavy duty garbage bag. There was a note attached attacking her in the same old way."

Linda Samuels leaned over and whispered to Angela.

"What does she want? A new way?"

"What about the dog?" the basketball coach called out. Usually the coaches didn't come to faculty meetings and if they did, they usually fell asleep sitting up, but by now the Sally crisis was even pulling them in.

"Dog peed on my foot," Angela said. Everybody looked at her.

"She was naturally distressed," Sally said, breaking her usual silence.

"Dog's fine," Helen said to the coach. "But I wanted to warn those of you who own dogs to keep yours inside for a few days. Someone out there is dangerous and unbalanced."

"They still think it's one of us?" Jennifer asked.

Sally smirked.

"We don't know," Helen said and then a tiny puddle began to form between her feet. She sat down but she couldn't control the flow anymore. Her bladder evidently had become too full and had taken on a life of its own.

After the meeting, teachers stood around in groups near their cars and, even though it was against the rules, began to seriously speculate about the identity of the perpetrator. Some thought it was a student who'd cracked under the excessive and rigid demands of Sally. Others thought it was Helen or Sister R. J. being threatened by Sally's height and natural authority and because she was critical of the administration. Angela's name was mentioned as somebody with motive (everybody had heard her bitching about Sally's vicious department meetings), but was immediately dismissed because of her rational character and timidity. One of the social studies teachers brought up the most interesting theory of all: that Sally was a multiple personality and the perpetrator herself.

Everything seemed absurd and nothing did. Somebody was sending notes and kidnapping dogs. Just the act of doing that was insane, wasn't it? Nobody came up with a viable solution but it was a relief to talk.

Nobody knew that Sally had stayed behind to work except for Linda Samuels, who was keeping it a secret. If they'd known, Helen and R. J. would have made her go home and that really ticked her off, giving this sociopath so much power. That was just what she wanted anyway, wasn't it? To know that Sally was scared, forced off campus. And besides, what danger was there really? Some kid (or adult maybe) she'd pissed off teases her dog, writes bad confessional poetry on bathroom stalls, watches too many made-for-TV movies, probably has mean parents, crummy posture, acne, and dyslexia. Well maybe not dyslexia, that would have shown up in the anonymous letters, but definitely too much time on her (or his) hands.

Sally smiled. She was so not threatened, she actually felt a little bit of compassion for the loser.

She was staying late in the windowless video room next to the library where the faculty meeting had been held to edit some tapes her students had prepared for the campus TV station about this controversy:

Pro or Con? Should athletes be allowed to wear their letter jackets to school every day?

Pro: Yes, because other clubs wear theirs.

Con: No, because sports have nothing to do with the school day.

Sally loved debates and she loved editing them. She told the students they couldn't do it themselves because the editing equipment was too delicate and valuable, but really it was because she secretly skewed the arguments so subtly that not even the actual debate team could tell what happened. Today she added a three-second pause before Sheila Campbell's first point against the jacket to suggest tentativeness and indecision. She also cut pauses from the pro side and removed an entire rambling, silly comment by Jessica Reynolds about how cute the jackets made team members look.

She blurred some of the audio section of the con debate, dubbing over one part of their best argument about recreation versus hard work with offstage coughing, a sound she kept hidden in a locked desk drawer for use when debates got close.

Why was she on the side of the athletes and their jackets?

Because if you bothered to read the uniform rules carefully you couldn't find a thing to base a denial on. It was all in writing, as clear as that. And besides, Sister R. J. had made her moderator of the athletic club and if her kids wanted to wear jackets, she'd see to it they could.

Sister Rose James hadn't been able to engage in any of the post-meeting gossip she saw going on in the parking lot which annoyed her. If she was going to solve this thing, she needed to find out what the faculty thought was going on. Still, if she'd stayed they wouldn't have talked about the case anyway, not with an administrator there. Helen had nixed that.

So as usual, she drove straight home, fed Prissy, and poured herself a big goblet of wine. Then she did something so perfect, so wonderful, that from this moment forward, she could hardly remember what her life had been like before.

She turned on the brand-new computer a salesman in her parish had gotten for her at cost and found the Internet. It was as easy as the science teacher had told them it would be during a recent technology in-service at Maryfield. From there, as if guided through the puzzles and pages and graphics by God Himself, she found herself in a strange Catholics' chat room where she introduced herself as Mona, a Dominican nun with a fondness for true crime and bondage. She was the immediate hit of the group, not one of whom actually believed for a moment that she was really the person she'd described.

Angela hadn't planned on talking to anybody gathered in the parking lot after the meeting, mostly because she was certain that they were all talking about her, speculating on her motives in the Sally situation. But to get to her car, she'd had to walk close to a group of teachers who called out to her to join them.

"So who do you think is doing it?" Gabe said.

Angela threw back her head and laughed out loud, a guffaw so broad all her teeth showed at once. She'd never laughed like that before in her life.

"Well, Helen's been acting pretty weird," she said. "Did you see her wet her pants at the end of the meeting?"

"No motivation," Serena said. "She likes Sally, doesn't she?"

"She's always weird," Rick said. "I heard from the janitor that she rubbed up against him one time last year. Pretended she'd slipped."

Angela got off of Helen. Accusing somebody else might sound like a diversionary tactic. Might sound like she was trying to throw them off of her.

"It's probably all the tension from the Sally Hamington thing catching up with her," she said, about Helen's behavior at the meeting, and then immediately regretted it. Calling it the "Sally Hamington thing" sounded too cold and victim-blaming, especially in front of Jennifer and Linda.

"I hear the detectives are going to interview some of us," Gabe said. "Friends and enemies, I guess. Friends to finger the enemies."

Angela's foot suddenly slipped out from under her and she started to slide down the side of the librarian's Jeep Cherokee. Gabe caught her under her arm.

"Sorry," she said. "I lost my balance. No lunch. No time. Had bathroom duty and lost my appetite." She realized she was overexplaining again like she was guilty of something or afraid.

"Here, have some Cheetos," Jennifer said. "I swiped them from the meeting. You guys can be my confessors."

"I can't stop eating," said Serena. "It's all this crazy stuff happening. I ate three doughnuts this morning. Didn't taste a thing. That's about seven hundred calories of pure sugar and fat."

Angela looked at a Cheeto and then, meditatively, sucked all the cheesy salt off the outside. She decided to be calm. Why not? So the detectives were going to interview her. So everybody in the school thought she was an insane secret criminal. So what? She hadn't done anything except not like Sally Hamington.

"What about you?" Rick said. "How's this whole thing affecting you?"

In fact, she might as well take the offensive. She'd come clean.

"I keep thinking you're all sure I'm the one who's doing it to Sally because I'm always complaining about her." There, she said it. They smiled warmly at her. They liked her or they were pretending to, just to find out more.

"She's been talking about you, too," Rick said. "Says you don't use lesson plans, that you don't give enough tests, that you don't follow orders."

"Really?" Angela said. "Well, I've even fantasized that she'd resign." She refrained from describing her other fantasies, of taking an ax to Sally's neck, putting nails in her tires, poison in her coffee.

"Fantasizing and acting on the fantasy are two very different things," Serena was saying placidly. "Fantasy is basically an outlet for the powerless and frustrated. I mean look at you. She got assigned to be department chair right behind your back. She probably campaigned for it. Then her first act is to ask all the other departments what you'd been doing wrong."

"The powerless and frustrated also write anonymous notes," Linda Samuels said. It was like she'd slapped Angela in the face in front of everybody. She'd gone over some invisible boundary accusing somebody in the group.

That was another crazy part of the scandal. You never really knew who you were talking to. Like now, here they'd been standing around talking after the meeting like pals and all of sudden people were thinking that one of them might be the perpetrator in disguise.

Sally had just leaned back, pleased with the preliminary results of her editing, when she heard the knock on the side door. She hesitated for a moment until she remembered that Linda had said she would be working late too. Probably she was checking on Sally, wanting to talk. They were sort of friends; they'd gotten closer during this anonymous letter thing. It gave them a way to trash Helen without having to reach too far.

"Hi," Sally said to her side of the locked door, just to check. It was of double thickness to safeguard the video and television equipment inside.

She heard a muffled "hi" and opened the door. It was a moment she'd replay hundreds of times after that, when she was sitting at home, day after day, staring at the wall.

So far all Chuck Grossman had done to earn his per diem was collect hearsay. He knew for example that Sally had failed the interview section of the police academy examination. He knew that Helen kept trying to quit smoking and had had a couple of brief affairs with guys on the board; he knew that Angela couldn't stand Sally (for which he couldn't exactly blame her).

He was no psychologist but Sally was so stiff she'd probably sink to the bottom of a swimming pool if somebody tossed her in. And when he talked to her he always sensed that she was critical of his techniques and questions, like she could do his job a lot better than he with her hands tied behind her back. In fact, early on she'd actually suggested that she conduct a large part of the investigation. He'd nixed the idea immediately by saying that school insurance wouldn't permit it. But she'd held it against him, he could tell, from her voice and body language.

And, goddamn it, he wasn't a sexist like most of the guys he had known in the police force. Not that they were obvious about it. They didn't feel women up or make lewd and suggestive remarks. What they'd do is they'd talk to women as if they were children or interrupt them. Or if a woman had a good idea they'd wait until a man restated it before they'd bother to take it seriously. Even when he was a cop he'd never been like that.

His wife was the one who had made him leave the force. He'd started getting sores all around his mouth. Big painful ugly things that were first diagnosed as herpes, then hives, and finally stress-related boils, a medieval-sounding infection nobody gets unless nerves are shot.

What got on his nerves weren't the typical things that make people quit. Not too much enthusiasm in the take-down or emotional flooding, as the police shrinks termed it. One too many battered babies, skinned puppies, gang-related drive-bys, so that you couldn't sleep and actually wept on the job, secretly sobbing in the squad car.

No. What got to him was the fear of getting killed. Simple as that. He was afraid. None of his buddies ever talked about that. So he didn't either. Never. Except to Sophy, his wife, who understood in a flash. For obvious reasons. She was a cop, too.

He had told her about Sally, as much as he knew, and asked her opinion. Asked who would hate her enough to try to ruin her life, who would risk this much to drive her nuts? What about Sally Hamington would make somebody want to destroy her reputation, her job prospects, her sense of control? What made her so disliked?

"The very thing that would have made her a bad cop," Sophy said, combing her curly long black hair. "Too rigid. Too law and order. These people who maintain too tight a system, too harsh a code, people under them always revolt after awhile. It's human nature. Look at *Mutiny on the Bounty*. You can't squeeze people like that without repercussions. It's a wonder whoever it is has stopped at anonymous letters and dognapping. She's a lucky gal."

He believed her. She was the one who had taught him about sexism in the police force and practically everything else he knew about human nature. She was so smart he sometimes wondered why she'd settled on him.

So when Sophy told him four years ago that being afraid made him one of the most well-adjusted people on the force, but that well-adjusted probably wasn't the best personality type for police work, he slept through the night for the first time in weeks and quit the next day.

Tonight she leaned back on the bed, her hair flowing out from her head like a Pre-Raphaelite painting and said, "Let's do it now."

She turned off the lights and lit a candle. It was their usual Saturday night, out to dinner, baby-sitter for Anna and Tom, long bath, good talk, and then an hour of lovemaking by candlelight.

"You know what I want?" she said. Chuck climbed in under the sheets beside her and ran his toes down her calf.

"No," he said. There were about six things she liked him to do in bed, but he never guessed which one it was going to be on any particular Saturday night.

"I'd like you to be a girl this time," she said. "How about it?"

That was a new one.

He shook his head.

"No?" she said. She was surprised. He never refused her anything, not even when she got into those bathroom games last year. Those were a lot kinkier than this.

"What?" Chuck said. "Sorry. I was just thinking about something else."

"About Sally Hamington," Sophy said. She knew him. Once he got into a job he chewed on it until he got a sense of all the players, as if he were one of them almost, and sometimes, that way, he figured out motivation and perpetrator in a few days' time.

"Yeah," he said and they let it go at that. It was getting late and Anna had a soccer game at the crack of dawn. He didn't know what he would do to make Sophy feel like she was with a woman tonight. He'd play it by ear. He'd pretend to be Sally Hamington.

Sally was sitting in a desk chair with a gun to her head. She could feel it shaking slightly which, as it suggested the inexperience and nervousness of the gunman, should have been comforting, but she also worried that it might just happen to go off.

She'd been stupid to open the door when she heard the knock. She'd thought it was Linda, checking on her. The kid, short, maybe twenty years old with a ridiculous stocking over his face, probably the brother or boyfriend of somebody at Maryfield, had pushed his way into the room, knocking over a plastic ficus that was part of the video film set, and hissed, "Sit in that chair and shut up. Shut up; don't move, or I'll shoot."

At first it had pissed her off. Some kid in baggy pants and a T-shirt telling her what to do and pushing her around. She almost pushed him back. She probably should have but she stopped herself. You're not invincible, Walt had always told her when she got a cold after working too hard. She stopped herself. She'd failed the physical portion of the police exam because of her shoulder, not the interview portion like she'd told people. It was her loose shoulder that disqualified her. It was the fact that it might get dislocated in combat situations that had done it.

She'd failed the police exam. How was she going to deck a kid with a gun?

She sat down. He put the gun to her head. His hand was shaking. He was scared. Why was he doing this? Was some student paying him? Sheila Campbell? Or some teacher or parent? Angela Martin? What could be worth the risk? Did he need drugs? Was his girlfriend withholding sex until he did this to her teacher? Did he get off on threatening others even if the beef had nothing to do with him? But he wasn't some career criminal. The gun was shaking at her head. And he smelled like metallic, nervous sweat.

She was uncharacteristically afraid, even to talk. What if she said just the thing that set him off? Something he interpreted as a put-down? What girl hated her enough to have gotten him to do this? She realized that nothing in her life had prepared her to see this through.

His breath was near her ear. It smelled like cigarettes and mints.

"Why are you doing this?" she finally said.

"Shut up. Come over to the computer and write what I tell you to." His voice cracked. This was a prepared speech. Somebody had planned all this ahead of time, watching her, waiting for the right moment.

If he was going to tell her to write a suicide note she should take her time. Buy time. For what? For somebody to surprise him? For him to reconsider, find God, discover her humanity, his?

"You don't have to do this. You can change the way things are going," she said. "Somebody's coming back. Nothing will happen. You can tell your boss you've scared the hell out of me. I'll quit my job."

But she'd never quit Maryfield. And if she didn't they'd try something like this again.

"Move," he said. "Stop talking. All you teachers do is talk." He jammed the gun between her shoulder blades, hard. She stood up. He was just trying to scare her, just like the notes, the dog, the bathroom graffiti. He wasn't going to kill her. She'd act scared so he'd go away, knowing he'd done his job. She'd try to cry.

Alice Todesco was David Brand's last client of the day, evening actually, which was unfortunate because that's when he was most tired and she was work, hard work. In fact, sometimes he had to drive his manicured nails into the palms of his hands to stay awake, the irony of which was not lost on him, her being such a cutter, as they called it in the self-abuse industry. Sometimes he went home with welts on his palms that Tony would always notice first thing. Tony was an MD who worked with AIDS patients all day long and he couldn't turn off the vigilance for symptoms just like that.

"It's Alice Todesco again," David said, taking his hand out of Tony's.

"Put her earlier," Tony said, for the fifteenth time. "You are not a night person." He knew that all too well. They'd lived together for four years and every time they went to the movies David fell asleep on his shoulder. It was cute at first. Tony felt tender as hell the first couple of times it happened, but after that it began to get on his nerves. He wasn't this guy's daddy. It made him feel lonely in that dark theater watching whatever foreign film it was this time, reading subtitles and seeing all these sensuous, life-affirming Europeans eat and make love while he had this heavy head, like a tumor, balanced on his shoulder. It got so bad he thought of slipping an amphetamine in David's evening coffee before going out.

"She'd take a schedule change wrong," David said. "She'd take it as a rejection and she's already had so much of that."

"She's controlling you, baby," Tony said, for the fifteenth time.

"She's suicidal, Tony. She cuts herself because she's so angry at the world for taking her mother. You just don't understand anybody who would want to hurt themselves, or somebody who would want to die."

But Tony did. He'd helped at least a dozen patients die which was technically against the law in this state, but it wasn't as if the authorities really cared about these guys: skeletal, demented, covered with sores. Nobody ever got prosecuted.

Of course, their situation wasn't anything like Alice Todesco's. Theirs was about real pain, not some schoolgirl tantrum that tricked David into endless empathy. But Tony knew he might as well give up about that. What was the point?

Tonight, thank God, they weren't going anywhere, so David got to soak in his bath with lemon-scented oil and candles running along the edge. He lay back and closed his eyes.

Tony almost always had something going. David analyzed his hyperactivity as a compulsion, a running away from the awful demons of death he had to deal with all day long. Sometimes it got so bad, all the parties, and dinners out and movies and plays, he found himself wondering if they were too mismatched to be together. Sometimes, quiet and home were more important to him than being with Tony, which until this moment, lying like a puckered corpse in the bathtub, he'd never really formed into a conscious thought.

And what business was it of Tony's about when he saw Alice Todesco, the poor kid?

Vincent, Alice's father, picked her up in front of David's office building after her appointment every Tuesday night. Even though it was dark by then and in a residential neighborhood where hiding places behind bushes and parked cars were plentiful, she wouldn't let him wait inside the building; she'd thrown a sort of fit actually, tossing her books on the ground outside his car and banging her head against the mahogany dashboard until he gave up and told her he'd wait outside in the car at the loading zone.

Although Vincent had only met David Brand once, he'd talked to him on the phone several times over the years and David had seemed a sharp enough guy if a little bit effeminate. The bottom line was he probably saw a fatted calf in Alice and didn't want to let her go. Why else should the therapy take so long? But what could Vincent do? Alice adored David; if Vincent questioned the treatment plan, she might do something to herself worse than digging at the skin on her forearms.

Vincent sat in his green Bentley and smoked a cigar. Poor Alice. Poor kid. Daughter of a dead mother and an old, rich father. Somebody should have bought up the screen rights to the story of her life. Shirley Temple would have played the part in the 1930s. Now who could reach sixteen with that kind of round faced, dimply, surprised innocence? Some vampire slayer or party girl? Some teen alcoholic or sex kitten? He'd been with enough of those himself to know that sixteen didn't mean a thing anymore. Sixteen going on thirty-five.

At least he could afford to pay for a pansy shrink and a live-in housekeeper and a private girls' school for Alice. And without fail, unless he was away on business, he picked her up after her appointment. Hoping, just hoping, she'd decide to tell him why she kept digging into her soft sweet skin with anything sharp she could lay her hands on.

"Hi, Daddy," she said, climbing in beside him. "I think David almost fell asleep tonight. He gets too tired at the end of the day."

Vincent pulled the car into the traffic. Tired? he wanted to say. From doing what? Sitting on his backside listening to people complain about their lives? How tiring could that be?

"So don't pay him," he said.

"It's my fault," she said. "I'm boring."

"It's his job. Change your appointment time and if it doesn't get better, change therapists."

"Daddy!" she said. He glanced over to make sure she wasn't digging a key into her forearm or something. Why couldn't they just talk it out like normal people?

"What?" he said.

"Well David, he's like a big brother to me, or a . . . ," she stopped.

"A father?" Vincent said.

"No, not at all," she said quickly. "He's a paid professional. I'll refuse to pay him for this session if that makes you happy." She wouldn't of course. Vincent wasn't stupid.

And from then on, all the way home, past the huge hallucinogenic billboards on the Sunset Strip advertising Tina Turner's thighs and the newest movie about adults turned into big children or children having to act like adults, through the winding gated streets of Beverly Hills to their home at the top of the world with 360 degree views of LA beaches, deserts, and mountains, neither of them said a word.

When Helen got home from the faculty meeting she stripped off her wet underwear and stockings and threw them right into the laundry hamper. She put on an extra large nightgown she found in the back of the closet that she'd forgotten to toss out the last time she lost a hundred pounds. She spent nearly every cent she had on clothes; sometimes she wondered if that was a subconscious reason she'd gained and lost 100 pounds so many times, so she had an excuse to buy a whole new wardrobe. She favored the same look, fat or thin, an exotic, sensuous layering of expensive silks and dyed fabrics. Things styled, cut, and decorated by human hands. She liked the idea that dozens of real people had labored over the act of clothing her.

She knew it wasn't good to smoke or to gain and lose weight the way she did. Especially when her job put her in the public eye, where she was supposed to present a moderating and mentoring influence on young girls and raise money and enrollment. She just shouldn't be so out of control of her own appetites. Plus, it wasn't good for her heart to yo-yo the way she did; all the nutritionists and physicians she'd been to had told her that.

But what choice did she have? Her body wanted those pounds, it craved them; she had a terrible snaillike metabolism and sturdy peasant legs with no visible ankle to weaken under the bulk. Her body wanted the weight and already only a year and a half after achieving her ideal weight for the fifth time in her life she was beginning to take on her usual look of a human pyramid. She waddled when she walked.

What choice did she have? She'd go to a new hospital, sign up for yet another medical weight loss program, lose another hundred pounds, buy a new wardrobe to show off her waistline and hips while they lasted, get a bunch of photographs taken to send to friends out of town and use for school publications, get a new driver's license, find somebody to have sex with while she looked OK, before he'd get that incipient panicked expression on his face when she rolled over, for fear probably that if she rolled too far, she most certainly would smother him to death.

Ah, fear of women's flesh. She was flesh incarnate, struggling to break free. That's why she loved the water so much, why she intended to save up to fly to a Club Med in Cancun or somewhere this summer where the native women were fat and the water was warm and clear.

Sally still couldn't cry even when he poured warm red stuff he said was animal blood over her head and shoulders from a flask he'd brought. She'd tried everything. Thinking about the belt beatings her father used to give her when she was five because of some little thing she'd done, like hide her vegetables under her plate at dinner or spill syrup on her Easter dress: something another parent might have thought of as charming or creative even, like squeezing mustard in a swirl pattern on the linoleum in the kitchen or sticking thumbtacks in the bottom of her loafers to see what sound they'd make when she walked on the tile floor. What a son of a bitch he was. When she was six her mother told her she was adopted and she'd said, "Good."

"Why, dear?" Her mother was a tall woman herself who had great difficulty with physical affection. The most she ever touched Sally was with brief pats on the back of her hand.

"Because I don't think anybody who was my real parent would be so mean."

"Move," the nervous kid said now.

Sally tried to think about the baby she'd never have if he killed her. Walt would be OK. He'd marry somebody else before the flesh had rotted off her bones. Not that he didn't love her; it was just so clear to Sally now that she was thinking about it, the kid's goddamn gun shaking at her temple probably about to go off anyway because he was out of control with fear, that Walt, with his bald spot growing larger like a spreading fungus every day, needed a strong woman around him to survive.

But a baby. Never until this moment had she even considered having a child. It was a surprisingly pleasant thought. The baby would be an easy delivery; Sally knew that; she was strong and athletic, and it would please her from day one, no power struggles, no tantrums, no skills problems, no girly-girl dramas like the girls at Maryfield; the baby would be just like her: smart, cool, reserved.

"Sit here, cunt. Write what I say."

Sally sat in the chair in front of the computer screen and put her hands on the keyboard. She was this close to using three or four karate moves to end the thing right now. This close. But all the other stuff came rushing in: "He's got a gun; don't fight, don't fight," particularly if he's shaking like this boy was.

"Write that because of my pedophilia I've decided to kill myself."

"You're kidding," Sally said. Suddenly she wasn't afraid anymore. This was all just too absurd. "You think anyone will buy that? Everybody knows this whole thing, the notes, the dognapping, is a con."

"Shut up," he said.

"This isn't TV," she said. "This is real."

"Shut up," he said. He was still pointing the gun at her, but now he was standing behind her, holding it to her back, right between the shoulder blades, so he could see the screen.

"The content of the notes, the pedophilia, isn't real either, even though by now you and your girlfriend probably think it is." She was typing this on the screen instead of what he was telling her. She paused. He didn't stop her. "That happens to sociopaths over time; they begin to believe their own lies. But you're not like that, are you? You know the score. You got manipulated and now you're realizing you've been screwed. You've been had. You're putting your life on the line for some girl who got an F she deserved. But listen, to me you're not here, OK? You walk out that door with my back to you and you're not here. Never have been."

He didn't go. He pushed the gun into her back again.

"Erase that. Write what I tell you."

She did. When she was finished he tied her up with the clothesline he'd brought. Then it was silent. Then there was a scraping noise outside. They both heard it. The kid jumped. She turned around.

"Run away. I hear a noise," she said right into his scared face. "Run away. The coast is clear. Run, run, run before it comes back."

He did. He ran out of the room, out the same door he'd come in. A couple of minutes later the sound came back. Sally recognized it. It was the sound of neighborhood kids skateboarding down the hall. The little trespassing bastards had saved her life.

Sally's husband, Walt, was drinking a Dos Equis at the picnic table in the backyard of the house. She'd said she'd be home about 7:30, after the worst of the traffic, after she'd finished editing some school debate, so he had time to have a couple beers and maybe a joint before she drove up. If not, he could always toss the bottle into the garbage can when he saw her lights in the driveway. She'd never find it. His household jobs were garbage, cooking, and toilets. Her jobs were laundry, auto repairs, and gifts for the family. She was the skin and brains, he was the plumbing, the guts. They never overlapped.

Walt burped, a long, low, loud one. He rarely drank in front of her during the week and she didn't have a clue about the dope, which Walt got from his brother in Oregon, who mailed him an ounce every six months or so, if they didn't see each other first, in a hollowed out hardcover book, a short classic usually, like *The Great Gatsby* or *A Tale of Two Cities*.

Tonight he'd finished three beers and an entire joint by the time she drove in. Maybe it was the joint getting him paranoid, whatever, he'd begun imagining her in a horrible crash, mutilated, paralyzed, burned beyond recognition, dead. And just at the moment he stood up to try to figure out what the hell he should do now, she drove up.

When he stood, Walt realized he was really pretty drunk. Sally walked right past him into the house.

He waited in the doorway and listened. She was taking a shower. He tossed his beer bottles into the garbage can, called the dog, and went inside.

He remembered seeing a TV movie where the first thing this girl did after being raped was take a shower. Same as Sally, exactly. The girl came home, walked inside the house without saying a word to anybody, and got into the shower with all her clothes on. The clothes part was obviously a Hollywood touch. Sally would never wear clothes into the shower, raped or not, but just the same never before had she walked past him without saying hello.

"Sal," he said into the bathroom. He figured he might as well brush his teeth while she was in there. He probably smelled like hell. Maybe he ought to toss a little water on his face, too, to sober up.

"Yeah," she said. "Sorry I'm late. The editing took longer than I expected."

He watched her through the glass shower door. She had a great body. Long lean legs and torso, nice big breasts, everything in proportion, all muscle but not sinewy. Walt loved her body. He dreamed about it.

"Wash my back Walt, OK?" He leaned in. He loved it. Her. Sally. He washed her back with the washcloth. He thought of moving down her butt but he didn't dare. If she'd wanted that she would have let him know it. But she didn't. She just stood there letting the water hit her face and chest.

"You OK?" he said.

"Sure," she said. And then she did something she'd never done before, something he couldn't ever imagine her doing in a million years. Something that shook him to the core. She leaned back against his hand and then she folded in upon herself and slid to the floor in a dead faint.

Later, after he'd done everything he could remember from first aid class, she stood and went into their bedroom and climbed into bed. No pajamas, no nothing.

Then she told him everything: the notes, the dog napping, the lawyers, investigators, and forensic shrinks. She'd never mentioned any of it before when she'd been pretty sure it would all go away. But now she knew it wasn't going away any time soon. If somebody was willing to risk making a kid hold a gun to her head, no way was it going to be over soon. She told him about the graffiti on the bathroom door. Everything she'd been hiding from him for weeks, especially what had happened tonight.

Alice Todesco had hidden her last semester grades from Vincent for three weeks. He was so incredibly stupid about when they came out it was almost too easy. He actually used to think she only got report cards once a year until he showed up for back-to-school night this year and Ms. Hamington had to keep bringing up her grading policy and how she averaged grades to the hundredth of a point and how many thousands of a point each missed vocabulary word was worth.

To Vincent, the teacher did seem pretty obsessive about standards and details. In fact, he had nodded off right after hearing her say that grades came out four times a year and that if you wanted to succeed in life and contribute to society you had to do your homework and keep track of your own grade point average at all times.

He hadn't gone to college so what did he know? He was a wealthy and successful commodities broker; he drove a Bentley and could afford to have sex with anybody, any way he wanted. So some people got lucky and didn't need anything but their own good instincts to rise to the top. But little Alice, he knew about her. What chance did she have, even with a college degree? She had no instincts about anything as far as he could tell. The most she could hope for was to be a librarian or a clerk. And she'd probably never be able to handle regular jobs like that anyway, because she was so high strung and sensitive.

He had never told Alice this, of course, not in so many words, but she got the picture. He thought she wasn't much. She knew he loved her because she was his. But, as they say, he didn't like her. Well, not that he didn't like her; he didn't respect her.

Alice could tell he worried about her. She could tell he didn't think she could get very far in the world without his help. It made her mad. It made her want to stick a big sharp pencil lead into the palm of her hand and dig around awhile until the lead and the blood made contact and maybe she'd get lead poisoning. She wanted to show him what she could do without him and without David, too.

The trouble was that her grades kept sucking and she kept having to hide her report cards until Jeremy Abbott, the nerd who lived next door, could fix them. He had a wicked crush on her so he would have done it for free, but she insisted on paying. She didn't want to have to owe him anything later.

She didn't know how Jeremy did it, something to do with accessing the school's database and rewriting her report card. She was always worried that it wouldn't work in the long run, that some counselor would take note of her sterling grade average and blow apart the entire scam. But the best thing that Jeremy could do—and this was the part that cost $250 a pop—was that he could get the doctored report card mailed whenever he wanted, weeks after the original one Alice had intercepted had been sent. Which was after all the counselors had looked them over and advised her to "Stop being such an underachiever. Think about the future. Think about your life."

Her father thought she was dumb anyway, even with those A's and B's. So did all her teachers at school, especially Ms. Hamington, who thought everybody was dumb except for a couple of kids who were completely engrossed in their schoolwork as well as being superior ass kissers. They did really sick stuff like turning in their big projects days early and typing when it wasn't necessary or offering to do extra research for no extra credit.

Alice sat down on her pretty white and yellow eyelet bedspread that she'd ordered from a bed-and-bath place on Rodeo Drive and started writing in her secret, secret journal (decorated with smiling bears and pastel angels) all about the fantasy character she'd created out of all her secret needs and hollow places inside. David didn't even know about it although he'd coined the term hollow places to use when they talked about how Alice mostly felt inside after her mother died.

She wasn't lazy and she wasn't dumb; she just didn't ever feel like doing much except this: writing and thinking about little stories starring her and her made-up character, the tall lady who ran her classroom like a marine but on the inside was soft and gentle and wanted nothing more than to spend all her free time with Alice going to the movies or out to lunch or shopping for pretty clothes they both could wear. Sometimes they'd go away for the weekend and the teacher would tuck Alice into the hotel bed and once in a while, a very, very, very long while, the teacher would climb in too and hold her warmly against her big soft breasts.

Angela drove to the bookstore/coffeehouse on her way home from the faculty meeting to check on the sales of her self-published poetry chapbook, *HeartMurder* (one word, like a rapid pulse). The store had kindly agreed to sell copies for her which was officially against policy but because she was a local and a frequent patron, they bent the rules. Only two copies had ever been sold, both to Angela who had given them as gifts, but she was still hopeful. Somebody attracted by the heart motif on the cover might impulsively pick up the book while wandering through the poetry section. And after reading a couple of poems, they'd be compelled to add it to their stack of purchases. Most of capitalism was based on variations of this scenario. It just had to dribble down to her.

Plus, she wanted to look at a dream analysis book to find out what it meant that she'd had a sex nightmare about Sally. She knew it couldn't be anything about sex.

She walked over to the Psychology section and found a book called *Secret Symbols in Dreams*. She took it off the shelf and, turning her back to everybody else in the aisle, opened up to "Female Sexuality." Right there in black and white she read:

> Good sex with somebody bad isn't about sex as much as the wish to incorporate certain personality traits of the lover into your own character. For example, if you dream about sex with a bank robber your psyche may be telling you to be more generous with yourself. If you dream about sex with someone you dislike, ask yourself what about this person you need inside of you.

Angela slammed the book closed. The woman next to her, reading about gambling addiction, jumped and dropped her book on the ground.

"Sorry," Angela said and bent over to pick it up for her.

She noticed that the woman was crying.

"Life is so difficult, isn't it?" Angela said and patted her on the shoulder. "Sometimes the best thing to do is to open a book of poetry and forget about self-improvement entirely. Just let yourself get swept away on the wings of verse, if you know what I mean."

And then she turned and slowly and deliberately strolled across the store toward *HeartMurder* where she did what she always did, opened her own book and pretended to be freshly moved by the dedication (to Sappho), thrilled by the meter (sapphic), and delighted by the woman-loving images, emotions, and ideas expressed by Anna Martinez, the poet.

> Frankly, I wanted her to be dead
> When she left. She wept a good deal
> And yet said to me—I must go.
> I admit it, I prayed to Aphrodite
> That she slip on a wet rock
> And crack her head open like a
> Ripe melon in August.

Angela didn't think anybody at Maryfield, except for Serena, to whom she'd given a copy and sworn to secrecy, would ever see the book but she'd used a pseudonym, just in case.

The last time she'd had a lover was Suzanne, disguised as Susan in her chapbook. They'd had a mostly sweet relationship which culminated in Suzanne's gay activist demand that Angela "come out," at work and everywhere else. Like she had any idea how difficult that was and how dangerous at a Catholic girls' school. Like she'd ever introduced Angela to either of her parents.

When Angela refused, Suzanne moved out and wouldn't even talk to her until she changed her mind. That was almost four years ago. Of course she missed the touching, the intimacy, and Suzanne herself. But she'd learned to sublimate her loneliness and angst into her writing, like many great artists. She'd feel even better, of course, if somebody was actually reading it.

The bookstore was playing jazz and people were wandering around carrying steaming cups of coffee and glancing at book displays. Angela picked up all the copies of her chapbook, as she always did, and turned them facing out so the title would show. But this time, after counting them, she noticed that four of the nine that had been there a month ago when she last checked, were gone. Four people had bought *HeartMurder*!

After checking to see if they'd fallen behind another book or onto the floor, Angela made her way into the attached coffee house and ordered a double cappuccino to celebrate. She was desperate to tell somebody the news about her book sales, but who? Not the coffee person certainly, not anybody at work except for Serena. She'd have to wait until she could call a friend from home.

When the coffee was ready Angela sat down on the soft brocaded couch and sighed. She could imagine those four people at home, picking up *HeartMurder* to reread a favorite poem, maybe out loud. Maybe one of the chapbooks had been chosen as a gift for a grieving and betrayed lover or maybe a feminist professor was using it in a poetry seminar. The possibilities were endless. Maybe the next collection she published wouldn't have to be self-published because of the word-of-mouth success of this one.

"Why, hi," a man's voice said. She looked up to see who it was. That forensic psychologist, Dr. what, Brooks was it? The guy they'd hired at Maryfield to psych them all out. The last person she wanted to see right now. Had he followed her here because she was such a suspect?

"Dr. Brooks," he said, holding a big paw out to her like she was supposed to be delighted to see him. Why hadn't she checked out the room before going in?

"Dr. Brooks," Angela said. And as she shook his right hand, she noticed what he had in his left, a copy of her chapbook, *HeartMurder*. It didn't make any sense.

And then it did. She was such a suspect that her good buddy Serena must have spilled the beans about the chapbook to appease the detectives. Because it had the word "murder" in the title, that made her a big possible perpetrator. Everybody was so crazy about the Sally Hamington situation that they were fingering each other. Screw loyalty, friendship, and honor. Even eco-earthy Serena.

"Dr. Brooks," she said again and gestured at the chair across from her. He was evidently the insecure type who had to be called doctor. She decided to ignore the book, at least for the moment. Let him do the work. "Any news on the Sally Hamington case?" Just put it right out there, she thought.

"They don't tell me much about the investigation," Jerome said. He paused, smiling disingenuously. Angela smiled back. They were playing a coy little game.

She didn't believe him in the least.

"Well, then give me the perpetrator's profile. You must have come up with that."

"I was hired mostly to help all of you to deal with the disruption," he lied. He put her book down on the table, cover up. Angela was very proud of that cover. She'd had a friend draw a picture of two women pulling on one heart. It had come out really well, better than a lot of cover art created by regular publishers.

"So you've never thought about what type of person would harass her this way?" she pressed.

"Passive, introverted, a reader," he answered finally. "Thus the poems, the sophisticated syntax. Probably not violent. Thus the anonymous letters. Probably holding a grudge. Maybe because of grades. Strong negative transference to tall, assertive women. Maybe was abused as a child."

"Impressive," Angela said. Except for the fact that he was supposedly describing a student, it sounded a lot like her. She took a sip of coffee and noticed that her hand was shaking. She hoped he didn't see it. It was strange how being suspected made you feel like you were hiding something.

"We're getting close," he said. His eyes were sparkling at her, headlights on a deer. Angela tried to hold his gaze. She put her coffee cup back down and missed the saucer. It spilled all over the table.

"Shit," she said.

Jerome wiped off the edges of her chapbook carefully.

"Oh," he said, "I almost forgot. Would you sign this for me? Right under your pseudonym, if you don't mind. I think I have a pen somewhere."

And she did. And even if he'd only bought it because she was such a suspect, it was one of the high points of her life so far.

"Got to go," he said after she handed it back. "Here's my card. Call me if you want to talk about anything. Anything at all."

Dr. Jerome Brooks left the bookstore feeling very pleased with himself. What a great coincidence to have run into Angela while he was shopping for her book. And asking her to sign it showed her they were on to something. The interview had been inconclusive of course, but her tension was palpable. He'd definitely scooped the rest of the team, that was certain. Helen would be delighted.

When she'd called him in to help out he'd said yes mostly because he wanted to see her again after all these years. Luckily, only the school was nuts, not Helen herself. She was the same as ever, maybe more orally fixated, but still lovely as could be.

They'd dated right after college, before he went off to get his PhD. Like many unmarried Catholic women of her generation, the only kind of sex she'd allow them was fellatio and she never let him touch her at all. At first he'd liked it, he didn't have to do a thing but get hard which was practically easier than breathing in those days.

But later, the sex had started making him feel like a piece of meat. He'd gone into his own analysis soon after they broke up. He'd learned a lot of stuff there he used in his own life as well as in his practice which, at that time, was mostly with the hardened criminals, murderers, and rapists he saw in the prison clinic.

Through analysis, Jerome got in touch with his rage which was eased somewhat by the cathartic rush he got from listening to his clients tell their tales of mayhem and murder.

Not that he thought talk therapy would make them safe to release, especially the sex criminals. Not that he believed in rehabilitation. He did his job, which was basically a waste of taxpayer money, not because he believed it changed his patients, but because he liked to hear what the guys had done.

So every time a white person mistook him for a guard or told him they didn't have a problem that he was black or ignored him in a restaurant all he'd had to do was go to work. And it wasn't just listening to the guys' horror stories that helped him manage his rage. It was worse. Even when he knew they were guilty, he wanted to help them. He'd testify under oath to almost anything that would: self-defense, PTSD, multiple personality disorder. After all, these guys were the real victims, helpless casualties of faulty wiring and parental abuse.

Jerome drove through Jack in the Box on his way home for a couple of tacos and an order of onion rings. He was in no hurry. His wife had left him three years before and his private client calls (he'd left the prison system years ago) could wait. He pulled his car under a streetlight and began to eat. He thought about the fear in Angela's eyes when he'd told her about how close they were getting. She'd spilled her coffee, poor thing. Maybe she had been doing it; she was just the type, jittery and too insecure to stand up to Hamington's demands. Maybe he could solve Helen's case for her and be a big hero, just like in the movies. The problem was, he felt sorry for Angela. She was the victim, of course, not big tough Sally Hamington. If she was doing it, Angela had been pushed.

He ran some ketchup carefully over an onion ring so as not to get it on his pants. It was disgusting that he ate like this, like somebody who didn't have his life together in the least. What if a client ever saw him? He did vary the restaurants: Monday—Burger King or McDonald's, Tuesday—Taco Bell, Wednesday—Jack in the Box, Thursday—El Pollo Loco, Friday—a hot dog at the movies, Saturday—the coffee shop at the bowling alley, and Sunday—a frozen pizza at home.

Tonight at the bookstore, after finding Angela's book, he'd browsed in the Psychology section to see if somebody could inspire him to take charge. At least it would be a start. He was getting a big pot and probably his carotid artery was completely blocked. At the rate he was going, pretty soon they were going to find him, when anybody bothered to look, dead, slumped over his steering wheel, mouth full of a grilled McChicken sandwich or a Whopper or a greasy apple pie.

In the made-up cyber world she had created for her chat room, Sister Rose James, a.k.a. Mona, was a nun who lived in a convent with many beautiful and desirable young women. Did any of her chatroom pals need to know that there hadn't been enough nuns in the last twenty years to fill a convent, that she lived in an antiseptic boxy apartment with a declawed cat, that she'd long ago overcome her own powerful attraction to women, in habit and out?

She invented a gripping narrative: lonely nun struggling with sexual impulses instead of having deep and meaningful conversations with her Maker. They wanted details. She gave them self-flagellation using a leather dog leash after succumbing to the temptations of a Puerto Rican novice in the form of the novice's soiled underwear which Mona had fished out of the common laundry hamper.

Tonight Sister Rose James couldn't sleep. It wasn't the kind of insomnia that could be fixed by a couple of hot hours on the Internet chatting with some other insomniac.

Even under three layers of blankets her feet were freezing, as freezing as they'd been in the convent where Mother Superior had only given them one cotton bedspread and refused to turn on the heat in their cells to help them develop strength of will. What they'd really developed was chronic bronchitis and an outbreak of special friendships as the poor little novices hopped into each other's beds to try to get warm.

Of course nobody had ever climbed into R. J.'s bed, which was too bad. God knew she was heavy enough even then to give off plenty of heat for two.

Jerome tossed his last onion ring out the window in a gesture of resolve. It landed around a raised sprinkler head which he took as a good omen. Tomorrow he'd drive to the health food market and stock up for the week. No matter that he'd have to eat in front of the television set because he was all alone. No matter that his feminist intellectual daughter wouldn't speak to him ever since he supported a self-defense murder plea as an expert witness for an accused rapist.

At least his daughter had given him a reason. His wife, Stella, hadn't even bothered to tell him when she left for good. She was so anxious to get away from him, she hadn't even stopped to pack a bag. People told him he was lucky, that he should count his blessings she didn't want any community property. To Jerome, that was even worse. She'd outgrown him, she said in the note she mailed to him a month later. She'd outgrown the big screen TV and the microwave and the Wolf stove and the wines they'd collected in Napa. She was going to India, that cliche. She was going to study with the Mahariji and pare herself down to the naked truth and leave him with all the ridiculous trappings of the bloated, barren, materialistic Western world.

The real truth, although he couldn't prove it, was that she'd run off with a professional bank robber named Jim Taylor, one of the smooth-talking ex-cons he'd helped get released from the slammer, one of the ex-cons she'd complained about for hanging around the house too much. Star of India and Diamond Jim used to trade insults so provocative, so nuanced with erotic charge that any moron could have seen it coming, any moron except Jerome. He was too caught up in guilt for encouraging these sociopaths to stop by with their imported six-packs and expensive Scotch and marbled filets that he hadn't noticed a thing. He deserved to lose Stella and his daughter, too.

And now he knew exactly what else he deserved. Helen Blalock. He was going to drive right over to her house and, if she was still willing after all these years, he was going to get the best damned blow job there was.

Maybe it was the shock of seeing big strong Sally Hamington that did it to her, that made her lose every ounce of her better judgment, Sister Rose James thought. Sally had sobbed and rubbed her wrists and begged her to keep the "incident" (as she insisted on calling the attempted murder) secret, until she, Sally, decided it was time to tell somebody. It was her incident, after all. It had happened to her. She was the target of all this "terrorism" and "intimidation." And the gun-wielding kid had never intended to do anything more than scare her into quitting her job, which of course she would never, ever, do. That would be like paying a kidnapper ransom on receipt of the tip of a human ear or whatever they'd taken from that Getty heir years ago in Italy.

After saying all that, Sally had seemed to finally begin to calm down. The chatter was doing her good, giving her back a feeling of power over the situation.

R. J. had untied the thin clothesline cord from around her wrists. It wasn't very hard to untie. She didn't even need the steak knife she'd found in the librarian's drawer which made her wonder if Sally could have tied her wrists herself, then thrown her arms over her head so it looked like somebody tied her hands together behind the chair? Did you have to be double jointed to do that?

And how had Sally dared, using the pencil-in-teeth dialing technique, to tell her to come to school in the dark to rescue her when a maniac killer was on the loose? Maybe even on the grounds still watching them even as Sally sat in front of her, rubbing her wrists?

"Let's call the police," R. J. had said. "This gives me the heebie jeebies. Forget it's your incident. It's mine now, too. I'm here. The guy's probably put a homemade bomb in my car. He's probably about to storm back in here and kill us both." She'd read enough true crime stories to know you should never relax your guard.

"No," Sally had said, and then teared up again, which deeply moved R. J. She just melted when people bravely tried to hold back their tears, especially tall handsome ones like Sally. R. J. herself cried at the drop of a hat, particularly about the tragedies of the famous: Kennedy's assassination, Princess Grace's funeral, Princess Diana's funeral, a Carpenter's song like "Close to You" on the oldies station, featuring poor skeletal Karen.

"All right," Rose James had said finally. "But we'll call tomorrow, assuming we make it out of here alive tonight."

"I must be afraid of her," R. J. said to herself now, in bed with cold feet in the middle of the night. She'd never done the wrong thing on purpose in her life, at least not publicly. Maybe she had a death wish as well.

Prissy rolled over and began to purr. Could they send her to jail if the masked gunman came back and shot up the faculty during their in-service meeting the next morning?

Abruptly, she sat up and turned on the lamp. It was, for a moment, like old times when she used to feel the hand of God on her shoulder telling her to do something difficult and scary. She dialed Helen's number even though it was 3:15 a.m. It wasn't the police she was calling so she wasn't betraying her vow to Sally, but she couldn't endanger the faculty. She waited for an answer or at least a tape, but nothing. Ring, ring, ring. Ten or twenty times the phone rang.

R. J. put the receiver down. Where was Helen in the middle of the night? Had the masked gunman gotten to her, too? She sat and stared at the wall and tried to figure out what to do. Finally she decided that what happened wasn't her responsibility anymore. Now it was God's. She'd done what she could. She was only a human being, flawed and weak- willed.

And with that, she threw the cat off the bed and got herself a glass of wine. She turned on her computer and went directly to her favorite chat room. Being human, if she couldn't sleep she might as well have some fun.

The in-service meeting the next morning was supposed to be different from the faculty meeting the afternoon before. It was supposed to be about community: connecting, supporting, nurturing each other to heal the broken faculty spirit caused by the Sally crisis.

"One Family Are We," the big banner above the chapel door said in blues, reds, and greens.

The campus minister who was in charge of the playful portion of the morning had put together an ice breaker. Everyone was supposed to run around trying to fill in peoples' names next to categories like: "has more than one cat," "eats artichokes often," "loves the color blue," stuff that wasn't amusing in the least. Angela thought up new ones: "has suicidal daydreams," "cross dresses," "enjoys child porn."

She watched glumly as people dashed up to each other all over the room and screamed "Blue? Blue?" "Cats? Cats?" like they gave a good goddamn. They were all trying hard so Helen would notice their positive team spirit. As if it mattered. As if they could ever be one big happy family again with all this dysfunctional Sally Hamington shit going on. With people like Serena turning you in to the detectives. With forensic psychologists stalking you in bookstores. With your nights disrupted by sex nightmares about people you hate.

"Angela, you're not playing," Gabe said to her.

"Twisted my ankle," she said. She was sitting in the corner, grading work. She'd been in a foul mood since yesterday. Here she was feeling like the prime suspect in the case when all she'd done was to hate the bitch, like half the school if they were brave enough to admit it.

"I won. I won." Serena shouted like an idiot. There wasn't even a prize. Big deal. Angela looked back down at her grade book. She hoped Serena, the traitor, would notice that she was being snubbed.

The next thing was small groups, and of course Angela was put with Sally and Helen. The playful but enlightening task was to come up with group commonalities, no matter how obscure.

"I've got it," Helen said.

Sally was watching something across the room absently, her eyes unusually unfocused.

"You OK?" Angela said. Not that she particularly cared how Sally felt. In four years she'd never once asked Angela how she was feeling, even when she'd been in the hospital for a week with a burst appendix.

"Headache," Sally said.

"Listen to me," Helen was saying. "I've got a commonality."

They both looked at her. What a controlling dope. As if she knew one thing about either of them.

"None of us like to burden others with our problems, do we? We all deal with difficulties on our own."

Helen was so dense she probably thought everybody in the world was just like her or at least aspired to be. Angela looked at Sally to see what gave. Sally looked at her and for the first time ever, she actually rolled her eyes as if they were agreeing on an inside joke. Oh my God, Angela thought. There's a person in there.

Angela smirked back at her and rolled her eyes, too. She knew neither of them would have ever disagreed to Helen's face. They were both good girls at heart. Not that as kids they would have ever been friends. In school, Angela had been the type who'd nodded encouragingly at the teacher, who made her feel needed. Sally had probably stared with silent, sullen criticism, implying she knew tons more than they did but she'd never be so rude as to point it out. Sally made them think they needed her.

Now the dorky campus minister was forcing them to do some Catholic humanist ritual about starting the new school quarter with hope for the future, reverence for the past, and respect for the present. Blah, blah, blah. Angela hated this part: standing in a circle, holding the clammy cold hand of the creep next to her and repeating this meaningless, self-satisfied crap in front of a group of near strangers.

The funny thing was that she used to sort of like this stuff, before Sally Hamington came to Maryfield and she'd lost her innocent optimism. Now the only thing that made her feel better was when she glanced to her right and saw Sally standing stiff and unblinking, holding the hands of Rose James on one side and Helen on the other and realized that she was feeling much, much worse. During the "hopes for the future" part of the ritual Angela thought hard. She tried to imagine wanting something new. Maybe to publish another book of poetry or climb a mountain with a bunch of women or open a business selling solar something or design homes or make a film about underprivileged, pregnant, battered girls in the ghetto.

I have goals for the future, Angela thought. I want to keep my job and have Sally lose hers.

"Dear Lord," the campus minister whined, "we put ourselves in your hands. We ask you to forgive us our sins. We ask you to heal us, guide us . . ."

"We ask you to debase us, humiliate us, force us to eat shit," Angela whispered to herself. She could never understand why the Catholic Church was so mean to people. How could anybody possibly be born a sinner? And why did they make you feel so bad about yourself just for hating somebody else?

Two days later the teachers listened to Helen's hushed announcement about "the gun incident" and how because Sally and Rose James hadn't called her or the detectives or the police until the day after it happened, there was no clean evidence and, even worse, that they'd all been put in grave danger at the happy community in-service.

And on this same day, Alice Todesco (who'd signed up for Angela's modern novels class at the quarter) announced in a shaky voice that the night before she'd dreamed she had a penis at which point somebody else said that she'd always wanted a penis too, and then Annie Klinestiver, several months pregnant in her maternity uniform, declared that maybe if they'd ever gotten laid they wouldn't have to own one full-time.

Oh my God, Angela thought, not another weird dream. She wished she'd bought that book she'd picked up at the bookstore. Was the strange atmosphere on campus causing the entire schools' unconscious to explode?

She decided to try to use the jittery energy in the room to her advantage, to subtly get the kids to explore something tangentially literary, but what? They hadn't even started the quarter's syllabus yet.

She sat down on the edge of her desk and pretended to be unflappable and spontaneous. She looked at the poster on the wall that said "Minds are like umbrellas; they only work when they're open," and the one next to it that admonished everybody to "Question Authority," posters that Sally had suggested she remove before Open House because of their controversial nature.

"OK, OK," she said. "Let's talk about Alice's penis."

The class looked at her, surprised but not shocked. Expectant maybe. She had them. Now what to do with them? Where to go?

"It wasn't my penis," Alice said, but Angela wasn't listening. She was trying to remember something about Alice, whom she had taught only once before, in summer school last year.

She looked pretty much the same as she had then, still carrying the baby fat which, with long stringy brown hair pulled back from her temples by two silver barrettes, gave her a childish look. A sprinkling of pink acne across her cheeks. A sour downturn to her mouth, almost a perpetual pout. Angela was glad she wasn't Alice's mother. In fact that was it; her mother was dead. That was the thing. And then she remembered something else from a confidential memorandum sent to all the teachers at the beginning of each year about the students' chronic illnesses and troubles: Alice was a cutter who had to be watched.

It was clear she liked saying the word out loud in class. Except she said pen-is, like the writing instrument. That made everybody laugh and made Angela have to corral them all over again.

"So whose was it?" she said. Huge laughter again but at least the teacher was winning the battle of the comedians.

"It was a dream," Alice said. "It was a symbol of something in my unconscious."

"Exactly," Angela said. "Perfect. And that's what this term in English is all about. The figurative level of literature, what's going on underneath the plot, the psychological secrets, the little lies, the symbolic meanings of castles and chairs and beetles and moonlight." On and on she went previewing books, reviewing others, and finally, brilliantly, dipping back into Alice's penis dream and guiding the class, with dignity and delicacy to help her figure out what it meant.

"Where was it?" somebody asked.

"The normal place," she said. "I had to have it removed. Big surgical procedure. My father held my hand."

Angela thought, be careful. Daddy's involved. Better terminate the discussion. Could backfire. Practicing psychology without a license.

"Wait. I know. I know," Alice said, still caught up in all the attention. "Penis-men-power-father-removal-ouch. Or," she paused, thinking about it, "pen-is wrong." Everybody laughed. Alice just sat there as the words sank in, staring straight ahead. No expression on her face. Why Alice, the troubled introvert had blurted out her dream was a mystery to Angela, but the important thing was that Angela had made it work.

Suddenly everybody burst into spontaneous applause. Angela jumped off the desk and applauded back at them.

Later on when Angela had time to think about it she wondered if her performance, her confidence and lack of inhibition, had been because Sally Hamington had gotten canned. But, not until the end, did she realize how connected to Sally Alice's dream was, too.

Sally Hamington hadn't exactly gotten canned. What Helen had said to them at the impromptu faculty meeting in those quiet measured tones was that for her own safety, for the safety of all of them, Sally was to remain off campus until the case was solved.

Not that anybody had many hopes for that. Nobody had a clue yet about the mystery notes and who was going to ever figure out the gunman's identity, out of all the millions of young men in the city? And Sally had already told the police she wouldn't participate in a lineup. She wanted to maintain a low profile. She wanted to keep her job; she wanted to be able to teach again.

So Helen once more forbade them to speak about it to anybody. And you could tell she was freaked out because of the way she kept wandering off the topic to stare out the window.

What Helen was picturing was the guerilla terrorist gunman sitting in an unmarked car behind a bush near the school entrance waiting, waiting, waiting to lob a homemade bomb right into Sally's classroom, maiming fifty kids and putting Helen's name in the national news. Not Sally Hamington's name, but hers, the irresponsible, naive high school principal, entrusted with the care of all those sweet innocent girls by loving parents who believed they could rest assured their precious babes were safe at least when they were in school; Catholic school, no less. That putting them into a Catholic school was as close as they could get to putting them into the outstretched hands of God, the white-haired, white-skinned, honey-breathed God they loved.

And Helen would be out of her job.

"So what do you think?" Chuck said to Jerome Brooks. They were sitting at a meeting with Helen, R. J., and Theresa de Cervantes, the school lawyer, after Helen's announcement to the faculty about the gunman incident.

Jerome took his precious time. Like he had all these big thoughts to distill into everyday words for the common folks. He probably just didn't have a clue or a theory so he was stalling in this pompous, grandstandy way. And Chuck wasn't being a racist, not like most of the white guys he knew from the police force.

While Chuck waited for Jerome to reveal his expertise, he took a glance around Helen's office where they were meeting. What a claustrophobic mishmash of fabric and sculpture and painting it was. Not little chotchkees you could knock over, but big stuff: a black and purple kimono displayed on one wall, a painting of three adult women with a book, bunch of balloons, and baby in each arm respectively, signed by Helen. An enormous dark vase on the floor, waist high, filled with peacock feathers and tree branches. Chuck suddenly felt if he sat one more minute in that room he wouldn't be able to take another full breath.

"Vagina dentata," Jerome said.

Chuck couldn't believe it. The room was filled with women, for God's sake. One was a nun and the other was single and Theresa, what was she? A professional mom?

"Pardon my Latin," Jerome said. "It's a Freudian concept which graphically describes his theory about the male fear of being smothered or consumed by the female, particularly during the act of intercourse." He looked around for reactions. Helen seemed amused. Sister Rose James looked absolutely fascinated. She was probably visualizing the concept, little nun teeth biting down hard. He'd perfected his theory after running into Angela Martin in the bookstore. It seemed to fit the situation pretty well.

"So what?" Chuck said petulantly. He'd have to ask Sophy about this one. She'd taken plenty of psych in college.

"So," Jerome said, knitting his fingers in front of his mouth. "That's how the perp feels about big strong Sally Hamington—threatened, smothered, overwhelmed. Yet conflicted. Drawn to her with irresistible force yet deathly afraid of being devoured by her strength. What to do?"

"What?" R. J. said.

"Do go on," Helen said. Was there the hint of a smile at the corners of her mouth?

"So what to do with the conflict? Blame the object of desire for causing it? No. That would be too close to home. Blame the object for something else. Perfect. Which releases the tension and resolves everything without demanding any reflection at all."

"So if you make the object of desire bad, you don't have to deal with the discomfort the attraction causes you," Theresa said.

"Men have been doing it since history began. Look at Pandora, look at Eve."

"Look at Hillary Clinton," Chuck said just to make a little joke. Nobody laughed.

"Sally Hamington is no Hillary Clinton," Helen said tightly.

"Go on," Jerome said.

"Sally is rigid, authoritarian, and humorless. I think she revels in making enemies of the kids. Thinks it means she is challenging them in spite of themselves."

"My daughters adore her," Theresa said. "They enjoy her clear demands and measurable consequences. But, of course, they're on the gifted track."

"Theresa's twins are in Ms. Hamington's ninth grade English class," R. J. explained to the men.

"Sally keeps secrets," Helen said. "We only found out after her mother died that she'd spent every evening taking care of her. Or that her husband had gotten laid off work and couldn't find a thing for six months or that her dream is to compete in the Olympics. And now suppressing information about this dangerous incident until the next day. Who knows what really happened?"

"Let's get it out on the table," Chuck said. "Are you saying she's been doing it to herself?" That would be the ideal solution, of course, if he could close both the case and nail Sally Hamington in the bargain. He'd rarely disliked the victim in an investigation as much as he did her.

"It could fit," Helen said, "as one possibility."

"Except that there's no motivation," R. J. said. They all looked at her, annoyed. Who was she to have an opinion about anything after what she'd done to set back the investigation?

"I called your house after I untied her," R. J. said. "I told you that. Nobody answered. At three in the morning. I didn't know what else to do."

"She could be a dissociator, a multiple personality with these warring parts cannibalizing each other," Jerome said.

Then Chuck and Helen and R. J. and even Theresa started arguing among themselves about the nature of Sally Hamington and the crimes that had been done to her and who was doing them and why. One of them brought up Angela as a potential perp; somebody else mentioned Sheila Campbell with the late term paper. And then there was a sulky parent whose daughter had been kicked off the debate team for being too mouthy. The discussion got so loud and heated that Helen had to bang her fist on the table to get them to calm down.

But Jerome wasn't listening. He was thinking about Helen and how soft her mouth had felt when she had touched him. How, even when the phone had kept ringing and ringing, like R. J. said it had, she hadn't stopped to answer it. She had treated him as if he were the center of her universe; her only desire had been to give him pleasure.

It hadn't been anything like that with Stella. With her it had always been "Does this feel good, darling?" "Am I going too fast, too deep, too hard for you?" And she was so particular about where they did it (bedroom, clean sheets), when they did it (during the day or with three dozen candles burning). And then, he was always having to tell her he loved her, all the way through the act.

He'd had to learn to pause (painfully and with exquisite self-control) to say "I love you, Stella," looking directly into her creamy brown eyes, and finally she'd smile back at him, take it in, never telling him she loved him by the way and then and only then could he ever so gently, a hummingbird fluttering into a sweet blossom looking for nectar, enter her.

"Jerome," Helen was saying now. "What do you think?"

He looked into her eyes and almost said, "I think I love you," before he remembered where he was.

"I think," he said and then hesitated. Chuck Grossman shifted in his seat. Theresa de Cervantes began to doodle on the legal pad in front of her. Rose James yawned luxuriously. Only Helen sat still, waiting patiently for his remarks.

"I think," he said, "that, as much as I hate to admit it, like most things connected to the murky minds of human beings, we may never find out the truth."

Sally's first sub was named Cynthia Nixon and everyone speculated that Helen must have gotten her from Central Casting. She was a meek, mousy creature, a clone of Sandy Dennis, quivering lips, red-rimmed eyes, every day wearing pastel shirtwaist dresses with a matching belt bisecting her narrow body. She stammered through Sally's classes and finally broke down and had to leave the room. Angela happened to be passing by and stepped in to sub for the sub.

"What happened?" she asked the class. She knew it wasn't a good idea to encourage the kids to tattle on the teacher. But she rationalized that the rules were different with a sub and besides she now had the official authority. Angela was back to being the department chair at least until Sally Hamington returned to work.

"She forgot something," said a freshman named Erin.

"The name of a Greek god. The one who adored himself in the pond."

"And what did you do to her?"

"Nothing," somebody said. "We waited quietly." She believed them. They were nice kids.

"Narcissus," Angela wrote on the board. Might as well teach them something while Cynthia Nixon was powdering her nose. When she came back they'd have a big laugh about hardening of the arteries. She'd align herself with Cynthia, two old crones alone in a room full of children.

But Cynthia never came back. She walked straight to her car and drove home without stopping. Then she called the school and told the receptionist that she'd realized teaching wasn't for her. She'd made up her mind. She was better with adults. She'd go back to her old job in the noncirculating section of the public library.

The second sub was a man named Aaron Brown who was a writer between jobs. Helen liked him of course because he was a guy and an artist. Over lunch in the faculty lounge, she'd mouthed, "He's a winner," to Angela.

But he only survived three days. It all came crashing down around him when he ridiculed Georgina Ramos for falling asleep during one of his interminable personal anecdotes about his tour of duty in Nam. She was sitting in the front row.

"Fine," he bellowed. "Go on, sleep. Your people probably never fought in a U.S. war. Probably don't pay taxes either. Sweet dreams while all of us real Americans do the dirty work."

You could see his spit flying even when he wasn't angry, but now it sprayed over poor Georgina's head into the face of Debbie Bennett in the second row who said, "Gross, Mr. Brown. You spit when you talk."

"And you smell, too," somebody else said. "Don't you wash your clothes?"

"Who said that?" he said. He didn't have to put up with this shit from anyone, least of all children. "Who said that?"

He was Aaron Brown, decorated in Vietnam thirty-five years ago, a screenplay titled *Courage in Action* optioned fifteen years ago, nothing since then except two lousy marriages and a brief stay in the locked ward of a small psychiatric hospital after he smashed a kid's face into the sidewalk one afternoon. The kid was six years old. Aaron had been watching him hide land mines in several pay phone booths. So what? The symptom of a little post-traumatic stress disorder. Everybody knew Vietnam was a nightmare. He got over it.

Of course he smelled. He was too busy to bathe. He was working on his new screenplay at night, after work, about war. Vietnam for the millennium. The war that was happening on the streets of America between the people who were born here, who contributed, and the people who walked over the border to have their babies and get free medical care and citizenship papers. The erosion of our way of life.

Georgina, whose father moved from Mexico to become the school janitor and a citizen, told her dad about what happened in class. He told her to forget about it. Debbie Bennett went to Angela.

But as much as Angela hated having to deal with these crazy subs and angry parent phone calls, the thought of Sally returning to harass her was much worse. That was her new nightmare.

When she received the note from Helen asking her to come to her office, Angela wasn't surprised. There were just so many subs the parents would accept before they started asking questions and even threatening to take their daughters out of the school.

"Sit down, Angela," Helen said.

Angela wasn't afraid of Helen but she didn't exactly trust her either. Helen had a way of pretending to be your pal that she found deeply suspect, like she was invariably softening you up to get you to divulge a secret or accept some ultimatum without a whimper. Today, Angela was betting on the former.

"It's been a challenge, hasn't it, running the department through all this instability?" Helen began.

"It's not too bad," Angela said noncommittally.

"I bet you hope Sally will be able to return soon, although I know you two have your differences."

There it was, sooner than she'd expected, the stinky bomb she was supposed to defuse.

"Of course I hope she'll be able to return," Angela said immediately, "when you think it's safe."

"Do you feel safe?"

Angela sat for a moment and for the first time really thought about it. Somebody had taken quite a chance to scare Sally or kill her even. Who could tell to what extremes a person like that would go if Sally returned?

"The perpetrator doesn't seem to want to hurt anybody besides Sally," she said finally.

"You know the perpetrator's modus operandi?" Helen said.

"Of course not. I'm simply stating the obvious."

"So if Sally returns before the case is solved and the perpetrator is found, she's putting us all at risk. Is that what you're saying?"

"I guess so," Angela said. She had a feeling she was being tricked somehow.

Helen leaned back in her chair and crossed her hands behind her head. "I need to tell you one more thing. The detectives are interested in interviewing you. Tomorrow, during your free period. Tell them anything that comes to mind. It's completely confidential."

"Just me?"

"People who worked closely with Sally, people who might have had run-ins. They're gathering information."

She thinks I did it, Angela thought. They all do. I'm still the best suspect. I'm probably the only suspect. They'll try to skewer me with it. Hang me from the cross. And I'm so suggestible, I'll probably help them. I'll probably hand them the hammer to do it with.

"Nothing to worry about," Helen said. She patted Angela on the shoulder to reassure her the interview didn't mean a thing.

When Angela got back to her classroom, she turned off the lights, locked the door, and put her head down on her desk. She was trying to stop the room from spinning. The idea that anybody could seriously imagine her writing nasty anonymous notes, hanging dogs from flagpoles, and hiring masked gunmen would have made her smile. If she hadn't wanted to cry.

Chuck Grossman was almost done with Sister Rose James. He'd been after her for nearly three hours and for half that time she'd been crying into the powder blue Kleenex Helen kept on her conference table. He had only one more area to explore and he was saving that for last.

"Sister, Sister, compose yourself," he said. He couldn't stand to watch her cry anymore. Of all the characters in his investigation, she made him the most uncomfortable. And it wasn't because he was anti-Catholic or anything like that. It wasn't because she was a nun and the first thing you thought of when you looked at her was how she lived without sex. It was because she seemed so vulnerable and pathetic.

"What you don't see is that I'll never get another job if I lose this one."

"Why would you lose this one?" he said.

"Because I let stupid Sally Hamington talk me into waiting to tell about the assault and then Helen didn't answer her phone. So they're blaming me for putting the entire community in jeopardy and ruining the evidence. I am an idiot, a weak-willed fool. I am too softhearted for this world. I have taken the gospel message too much to heart and now look what's happened. I lost sight of the larger picture because I felt sorry for Sally."

"Did she threaten you? Is that what you're saying?" Chuck wouldn't have put that past Sally in the least.

"Do you have any idea what they do to nuns who can't work anymore? They send you to live in the retirement house in the country. You live in this tiny room and pray and eat bland food and take care of the senile, incontinent ones until you get to be that way yourself. It's hell on earth."

At least she wasn't crying anymore, Chuck thought.

"I know about what happened at St. Ann's, Sister," he said gently. "But I'd like to hear about it from you." He was referring to a vague innuendo he'd gotten from Helen about the job R. J. had had before Maryfield. He waited patiently while she collected herself. He was trying to appear open and sympathetic, although it was tough. These nuns were all clearly psychotic, speaking to God, some figment of their imagination, some father-wish hallucination.

"Do you believe in God, son?" she said finally in a different, deeper voice.

"Of course, Sister," he said.

"Well then you'll understand that in my former place of employment I had no choice but to follow God's orders and tell this man, the faculty member, that I loved him."

"What?" Chuck said. This was more than he had bargained for. "You were asked to resign because you wrote notes telling some guy you loved him?"

"Sounds absurd, doesn't it? But it's true. He wouldn't listen to me at first. I'd watch him pull out my notes and show his friends and they'd laugh. I had to keep sending them until he understood. You see it was God's love I was offering him. God's love flowing through me. God was trying to tell him that although he was a homosexual He loved him anyway, in spite of it."

"So you were acting as a mouthpiece for God? You hear his voice and all?"

"The fellow figured out it was me sending the notes eventually but he tragically misunderstood my intentions and accused me of sexual harassment."

Chuck couldn't help but smile at the thought.

"He looked very much like you," R. J. said.

"Did he?" Chuck said.

"In a very cowardly homosexual way he went directly to the principal, behind my back, and tattled. I still believe this was at the prodding of his contemporaries in the faculty lounge. Left to his own devices, I believe he would have responded to me, but, as I said, he was a coward in the face of God's love."

"So, Sister, if God told you that a certain teacher was a pedophile and that she should be stopped, what then?"

"Why then I would have to stop the teacher, you silly man. Obviously."

Chuck Grossman looked at her, little repressed crazy mouse. This was almost too easy. He was so good at his job. He knew how to speak their language. He knew how to get inside their heads, these articulate crazy animals, this colorful menagerie called humanity, this fascinating bouillabaisse called life. He was practically panting with the thrill of the hunt and the impending kill. Forget Angela and Sheila and even Sally herself. Sister Rose James was the perpetrator. She was telling him that herself.

"But Mr. Grossman," R. J. said. She was smiling now, full of tricks herself. She'd seen his trap coming a mile away. "This time God didn't tell me about any pedophiles and He didn't tell me to write notes to anybody. This time God told me to leave everything alone."

Theresa de Cervantes was trying to get the waiter's attention in a subtle and inoffensive way by raising her left hand and bending it backward at the wrist. She'd seen somebody do just this in an old movie and it had worked immediately. She'd been trying to get waited on for five minutes.

She watched so many films from the 1940s that they had all kind of run together in her mind. The acting was uniformly broad and stiff; the plots were predictable and frequently racist but, the clothes, the sets, the privilege! She loved watching Lauren or Cary or Bette pad around in those white living rooms, smoking, drinking martinis, floating in from the garden after tennis or planting something ornamental.

To give them a taste of this old-fashioned entitlement, during their spring break she'd taken the twins all the way up the coast to tour Hearst Castle and from there to the Mark Hopkins in San Francisco. They ate oysters Rockefeller and filet mignon. They bought dresses at

Bergdorfs; they had tea in the lobby of the Mark at four o'clock in the afternoon. And those girls, her fourteen-year-old twins whom she loved more than anything, whom she loved so much she actually had to deliberately control her almost overpowering impulse to lock them in their room twenty-four hours a day to keep them safe, had enjoyed every minute.

She had the insight, just barely, to give them some freedom in this world gone mad. They took a regular car pool to Maryfield where they were in the ninth grade; they went to day camp in the summer; they went to birthday parties. But not sleepovers. Theresa was a DA and knew firsthand the kind of dangers lurking outside of suburban teenage girls' rooms in the middle of the night.

It had worked. Popular wisdom to the contrary, they'd turned out be miniature versions of her. Instead of sneaking off to get pierced and tattooed in the fist of adolescent rebellion like some of their class-mates, they'd become sophisticated aficionados of the good life filled with fine restaurants, boutiques in Beverly Hills, the opera, and the-ater and vacations abroad. And they did it all without a father. That hadn't been necessary, at least not after Theresa had found a killer sperm donor with brains and brawn to die for.

"Waiter," Theresa called out as he walked past their table. Was he ignoring them on purpose? She had cold coffee and Erin had a dirty fork. She was this close to making a scene.

The waiter, a middle-aged blond man, a man who should have been doing something better by now even though the tips were good in this swanky Italian restaurant, flew by them, eyes focused on some-body else, a table of men ordering another round of martinis.

Megan put out her foot. Unbelievably. With one delicious and ele-gant movement, hardly noticeable unless you were looking for it. And both girls had long long legs for their age so that the waiter did trip, stumbling forward and finally landing on his hands and knees, a prat-fall worthy of any Chaplin film. Theresa looked at Megan and winked. It was a bad thing she'd done; the man could have been hurt, but she couldn't help feeling proud of her daughter for doing it. She would most certainly go far if she could keep her impulsivity under control.

The waiter limped past them toward the kitchen.

"Could you send someone with a new fork and some coffee?" Theresa said to him. "Your replacement or a busperson?"

He knew. He wasn't stupid. But he could never prove a thing.

Which was, Theresa reflected, not to put too fine a point on it, the whole problem with life. Most people couldn't prove a thing. Nobody ever got the satisfaction of certainty; they just had to limp along, vaguely afraid and angry, confused and distrustful. Does God exist? Why am I here? Did O. J. really do it? Did my father love me? Why did my mother drink? And who was doing all the damage in the Sally Hamington thing?

It was the big reason she'd become a DA, not to see justice done or to exercise her brain or to achieve a big rush from winning or even because she loved to be on stage. She did it simply because she was desperate to know the truth. She had this hope (she'd almost never lost a case even when the police screwed up the evidence) that by the end of the trial she might come pretty close.

"Mom," Erin was saying. Theresa jumped. She was still a little nervous someone might have seen Megan trip the waiter. She'd have to reprimand her once they got to the car. Getting a fork and hot coffee wasn't worth the risk of a lawsuit. Still, at least now they were eating dessert so that Theresa could get everybody home soon to do their schoolwork. They were in Sally Hamington's English class and although those terrible subs were still trying to find their place in the textbook, the girls had plenty of math and science to do.

They got good grades from Ms. Hamington and had been learning a lot of valuable English material like vocabulary and literary terms they could use on their SATs, until the gun to the head incident had put an end to her teaching. The world was a wicked place, but Sally Hamington was no pedophile. Theresa had vowed to solve the case, thin though it was on evidence and eyewitnesses.

She couldn't have had better help. Megan and Erin were her secret assistants, her Watson and Bess, prowling around locker rooms, bathrooms, and the cafeteria line, observing their classmates and teachers when they could get away with it. She hadn't mentioned recruiting them to James or Chuck for fear of misunderstanding, but she knew kids and if any student on campus had been messing with Sally Hamington, they wouldn't be able to keep it quiet. When they started to brag about it, her Megan and Erin would be right there, quietly memorizing the facts.

But so far the twins hadn't turned up anything more substantial than some junior who'd spelled the principal's name wrong in the school newspaper and another kid, a black-haired sophomore, who was writing a one-act play in which the main character, the basketball coach, liked to take individual high scorers out to dinner at Shakey's alone.

It wasn't for lack of trying. Erin and Megan both wanted Ms. Hamington to come back to work ASAP. They were getting As but that wasn't the main reason they missed her. What they told their mom was that Sally Hamington was no BS, which they were allowed to say if they used only the initials. And the twins were good girls. They didn't even say the word behind Theresa's back.

After the "incident" as everybody was calling the fake suicide/ masked gunman event, Sally Hamington kept telephoning Sister Rose James, babbling harebrained theories about who was behind it all and badmouthing the investigators and Helen Blalock herself.

"Sally," Rose had finally said, "don't call me anymore. They might be listening in."

"Good," Sally said. She had nothing to lose. She was being paid her full-time salary to stay off campus. For Sister Rose James it was a different story.

"I think they suspect us or me or you."

She had to go to work every day and face people whose reactions ranged from fear to loathing to flat-out disdain. People whispered behind her back. Helen Blalock never spoke to her at all. Rose James had revealed poor judgment by not calling the police. She had ruined evidence. She had put them all at risk.

"How could they suspect you?" Sally said. "Someone whose only passion in life is the school dress code?"

It was almost true. Since the night of the incident, Rose James hadn't touched her computer. The chat room didn't seem dangerous and fun anymore. It seemed downright sordid. What she couldn't understand was how things had gotten so bad when all her life all she'd been was good.

A few days later, Helen Blalock and Theresa de Cervantes closed Sister Rose James' office door behind them and told her she was being let go, like a maid or temporary clerk caught with her hand in the till.

She'd known they were angry but she had no idea they'd ever go this far. She was so surprised that all she could think about was how lucky it was she'd just cleaned her office, tossing the towers of paperwork that usually sat on every available surface into a box.

Everybody sat down, the two visitors in chairs across from R. J.'s desk.

"It's for the good of the school," Helen said to her. Helen's wide mouth and big teeth reminded R. J. of Mr. Ed. Nothing else seemed real to her, not the young alumna lawyer sitting there in front of her desk looking disapproving, not what Helen was saying, not anything.

"I'm sure you understand why you're being asked to resign," Theresa was saying. Rose James was deeply offended. Who was she, this ex-student, to speak this way to her?

"After all these years of service," Rose James said. "One mistake. Where is your compassion, your forgiveness?"

"Please sign here," the lawyer said. "It's a statement saying you understand what's happening."

Now something was happening to R. J., but not what the young lawyer meant. It was something more powerful than anything she had ever felt before. It was like fear but not the kind that made you run away or cower either; it was the kind of fear that propelled you forward and as it did you realized it wasn't fear but anger, red hot rage that was moving you on and because of that, Sister R. J. took three steps over to where Helen was sitting, picked up her forearm like a giant drumstick and took a large sharp bite out of the tasty fat meat.

"Jesus Christ," Helen shouted and pushed her away. The wound was streaming blood. And was R. J. actually standing there in front of her chewing on a mouthful of her flesh?

A week later, Helen Blalock still felt like hell. Firing Rose James for bad judgment was the most unpleasant thing she'd ever had to do. Firing a nun was just above kicking a dog or teasing a child. And then, to have provoked such a reaction. She'd had to have a tetanus shot and twenty stitches to sew the wound up. The only good thing about it was that it proved what a nut case Rose James was, how unsuited for a job involving any responsibility for those more vulnerable than she. Rose James had turned out to be the most vulnerable of them all.

Of course, firing her didn't get them any closer to solving the case, but it had certainly stirred the pot. Helen had had to send a description of the "Sally Hamington incident" to the parents and students as an explanation for letting R. J. go. She hoped that, instead of causing a mass exodus, it might turn up a few new suspicions. Somebody must have seen or heard something.

And even if nothing came of it, sacrificing the old cow might have saved her own job. At least she'd acted with decision.

Helen coughed and wiped her mouth with a Kleenex. She'd had a killer sore throat since she fired R. J. It was so bad she couldn't even smoke. Looking out her office window above the terrace at arriving students and teachers, she still couldn't really imagine any of them being behind the attack. Except for maybe Angela who seemed to be happier than she'd been since Helen had known her.

She opened up the Kleenex and examined it for blood. She was almost sure she had throat cancer or lung cancer but she was too scared to go to the doctor to check it out. If it was cancer, she was a goner anyway. Nobody ever survived lung cancer so why bother losing a lung and receiving enormous amounts of chemotherapy to salvage a couple of lonely, painful months of life. She might as well keep smoking until she couldn't breathe anymore. Probably the cough, the sore throat, the cancer were a punishment for something, but damned if she could figure out for what.

Helen reached for the I-Ching coins which were hidden at the back of her desk drawer. Sometimes, in a pinch, she consulted certain divination tools, a practice she knew enough not to publicize at work. She threw them six times to find the hexagram that would tell her what to do next. Number 40, Liberation, advised her to act with firm, aggressive expedience. Amazing! She had done just that with Rose James. Her instinctual life was still right on; her sore throat wasn't a punishment after all. And as soon as she realized that, it began to go away.

Sally Hamington was going crazy, slowly but surely. She'd tried everything to pull herself together but here she was sitting on the pot, staring at the bathroom wall, watching her life go down the toilet. She could hear Walt pacing around the house, looking for something to do. She knew he was worried.

All Walt knew was that his whole life had changed with Sally around the house day and night. No more dope, no more buzzy greetings at the end of their day. He'd only been able to get a part-time bookkeeping job after getting laid off from the bank so he was around almost as much as she was. Now there were fights all the time about stupid shit: Word choice—"Are you saying that I'm insensitive?" Irresponsibility—"You never clean up the kitchen when you cook." Dishonesty—"Why didn't you tell me before about the anonymous letters?"

And unspoken underneath all this was his recognition that Sally was really very strange, that maybe she was even guilty of something and that she deserved the harassment she was getting. Innocent or not, the bottom line was, what did it say about the woman he married that she inspired this much hate?

After she came out of the bathroom, Walt watched her begin to write in the notebook she'd started keeping. It was as if he didn't know her. She was some high school English teacher who got anonymous notes accusing her of pedophilia, who'd been tied up, drenched with animal blood, and almost shot. But this view of her didn't move him to pity, instead it revolted him. It made her a freak.

"Why you, Sally?" he said to her now. It was Saturday morning and she was drawing some complex pentagonal diagram. Maybe she was certifiably mad, like Son of Sam, and he'd never noticed before. She looked up. She had a faraway reddish glint in her eyes.

"I'm diagramming possible perpetrators. My thinking now is that it might be a conspiracy, a group thing. The principal, the student council president, and Angela all got together to get rid of me. I think I can work this out on paper." She bent her head.

"But what's the motive?" Walt said. Maybe he would have to commit her like T. S. Eliot did his wife. Or Ted Hughes with Sylvia. Or George Sexton with Anne. Did husbands still get to do that? Did he have to prove she was a danger to herself and others or could he just show the judge her psycho notebook?

"Isn't it obvious? My strength, my opinions, my challenging assignments, my tough grading, my take-no-prisoners attitude, my disdain for hypocrisy, dishonesty, administrative bullshit, and waffling. If you're a loser trying to get by, you'll hate me. You'll want me gone. Get it?"

She was jabbing her finger into his chest. He pushed it away. She was pissing him off.

"And somebody made it work," he said, "and that's making you crazy. Somebody actually got you out of there. You're not invincible after all. It's like a Greek tragedy, isn't it? Proud yet cursed noble hero comes face to face with her fatal flaw."

She went for his throat, like she was an animal. He actually thought that thought, like an animal. Then, like the human being he was, he passed out.

When he woke up, he was lying on their bed. Classical music was playing in the background and there was a pleasant smell in the air, of citrus, of oranges. He turned his head and touched his throat, surprised that it didn't hurt. She had strangled him so hard with those big hands of hers that she'd cut off the oxygen to his brain, oxygen or whatever the hell happened when you got strangled.

Next to the bed was a glass of orange juice. It looked fresh squeezed, just like him, fresh squeezed. He smiled sardonically at his little joke. She'd made some juice for when he came to. Like that would fix everything.

She walked into the room carrying her notebook.

"You've been asleep for two hours," she said. "I was about to wake you up."

"Asleep? I was strangled."

"Walt, listen to me. You passed out from emotion, not strangling. I barely touched you. Look." She moved toward his neck. He flinched. "No marks. No pain."

"Don't touch me," he said.

"OK, OK," she said and sat down on the edge of the bed. "Wouldn't it be perfect if this crazy perpetrator succeeded not only in getting me laid off at work but breaking up my marriage as well? Wouldn't that be a laugh?"

Walt didn't say anything. He glared at her and waited for an apology.

She opened her notebook where she'd been writing down more of her crime theories. "I've been writing about my flaw," she said. "Want to hear?"

And only then did he begin to relax.

Alice missed Sally Hamington so much she'd started cutting again but she hid it from David so she could do it in peace. They'd let her transfer from Hamington's class to Ms. Martin's but that hadn't helped either. Nothing helped. She kept having these weird dreams about extraneous body parts and the only thing she could think of to do was to cut. She did it on the side of her feet, long thin lines that bled in stripes onto her socks, covered up by her school loafers. Of course she had to throw her socks out after each wearing or else Ginny, the new cook/ housekeeper, would find them and tell Vincent what was going on.

And then another bad thing happened, something not quite as bad as what happened with Ms. Hamington but worse than the usual stuff with her father. One night after a particularly hideous nightmare about giving birth to a squirming puppy, Alice got up and padded down the hall to her father's suite to see if she could get him to wake up and talk to her or watch TV or something.

She quietly opened his door and saw that he was awake already. The lights were on and he was lying flat on his back moaning, sobbing almost. But he wasn't having a nightmare like she had been. What he was moaning about was that Ginny was seated on top of him moving up and down ever so slowly like she was a child riding a rocking horse.

Alice gasped and they both stopped to look at her.

"Oh my God," Ginny said.

Vincent rolled over and she fell off of him onto the floor.

"Baby," he said, pulling on his silk bathrobe. "Alice."

"It's OK, Daddy," she said and she started to giggle. It was almost like slapstick; Ginny, the maid, lying naked on the floor; Vincent scrambling around. She thought of Desi and Lucy reruns, except this would have to be X-rated.

"Forget about it," Vincent said putting his arm around her and ushering her out of the room. "I get lonely sometimes. Doesn't mean a thing."

"It's OK, Daddy," Alice said again. She walked back to her bedroom and, after cutting deeply into her right calf, the only good place left, she lay down in the dark. But it wasn't OK. It was very bad. What he didn't get was that she was lonely, too.

After having another icky sex dream about Sally Hamington, Angela decided she ought to call her up and at least pretend to care about what she was going through. No job, nothing to do all day because she was in limbo about whether she was going to get to return to Maryfield and, according to Linda Samuels who talked to her regularly, no peace because she was so angry at Helen Blalock for keeping her off campus. For an obsessive like Sally, any one of the above was a recipe for hell.

Maybe calling Sally up and pretending to feel really bad about what she was going through would put an end to the sex dreams. Maybe if she saw Sally as a weak and shattered human being, she wouldn't have to keep metaphorically seeking to take in her strength, like the dream analysis book had suggested she was doing. If she acted powerfully, maybe her unconscious would believe she was.

On the other hand, maybe she just needed some sex.

Angela sat down on the green director's chair she kept in the kitchen and picked up the phone. While she dialed she tried to remember that one time she'd felt a particle of human warmth about Sally, at the faculty meeting when they'd been put into the ridiculous group with Helen. It didn't work. After the telephone rang three times, she hung up. If the tables were turned, Angela decided, Sally would never in a million years call her.

The next day Chuck, playing good cop, ushered Angela into Helen's office where he was interviewing staff and faculty about their take on the "Sally Hamington situation."

"We're sorry to interrupt your teaching day," Chuck said jovially, as if he really cared about how they'd inconvenienced her. He introduced her to Rex something, the bad cop he'd brought in to help with the interviews, who told her to sit down.

Angela was so scared she was hardly breathing. She was the lead in some film noir but she hadn't learned the script and she didn't know the subtext. She was praying neither of the detectives noticed.

"We're talking to folks who worked closely with Sally Hamington. People have mentioned that you didn't much like her." Chuck nodded at her with encouragement like he didn't think much of Sally either. Angela knew that was part of the strategy.

She'd planned on being calm, reminding herself that she had nothing to hide, but the way he brought up other people talking about her, the way they were both examining her, made her feel like every answer she gave was an evasion. She kept looking at herself from their point of view, which was a bad mistake.

"Well, at first we had some trouble. She became department chair and came down pretty hard on the rest of us."

"Hard?" Rex, a beefy older guy with an auburn toupee, barked.

"But we worked it out," Angela said. She leaned forward and rested her chin on her hands. She knew it was important for them to think she was relaxed and forthcoming.

"You worked it out?" Chuck said warmly.

She wanted to tell them she hadn't written the goddamn notes. She hadn't hired somebody to put a gun to Sally's head. She hadn't done a thing; she'd only hated Sally and been glad she was gone. But she didn't. She figured it was better not to dignify the unspoken accusations with a nervous, rambling denial.

"Oh, come on," Rex suddenly barked. "Admit it. You hated her. You got your old job back when she had to leave. Nobody breathing down your neck anymore."

Angela couldn't get her mouth open. So here it was finally. The whole moment was so theatrical and unreal. She was caught between an impulse to laugh or cry.

"You wrote her the anonymous notes, the poems. You're an English teacher. You can write." Rex was pointing a hairy finger at her. What a bastard. Could you sue a detective for yelling at you during an interview?

"Rex, Rex," Chuck patted his arm. "I'm sure Angela can explain." He reached down to the floor beside his chair and picked up *HeartMurder*. "We got your poems at the bookstore, Angela, and I must say we found them very interesting. Of course, we would never have read something like this except for this case. Not that we're homophobic."

"Explain what?" Angela said.

"Did you hire the gunman or was he a friend?" Rex said.

Chuck turned to one of her poems and began reading.

> Go tuneful Lesbian maids, and tell her
> How dangerous it is to hear that song of hers,
> And fatal to my heart to see those murderous eyes.
> Tell her to go away from me,
> Before one of us should die.

He paused and watched for a reaction. Angela sat still.

"You read poetry rather well," she said flatly. She absolutely refused to take the bait.

"Thanks," he said.

"She was all the time after you, wasn't she?" Rex growled. "Checking on your lessons, grade book, assignments, your correction code. She observed your teaching and judged you average. Not even good, certainly not superior, and you are superior, aren't you? Superior to Sally Hamington, that's for sure. All systems and rigid demands. That's teaching to somebody like her. Not an art like it is to you. And she wanted you fired!"

"She did?" Angela said. "How do you know that?"

"She told Helen that you were the weakest teacher in the school," Chuck said.

"So you got rid of her first," Rex said, saliva spraying into her face. "Didn't you, didn't you? You knew you'd never be able to land another job, not with a pornographic chapbook for sale in the local bookstore. Not once everybody found out about your lesbian leanings. Who wants a card-carrying lesbo teaching their children?"

Chuck pushed a piece of paper and a pen in front of her.

"Sign here," he said.

"What?" she said.

"It's a confession," Chuck said. "It will make you feel better."

Angela stood up.

"A confession?" she said. "You've got to be kidding." Suddenly she felt as tall as Sally Hamington as she towered over the two silly, seated detectives. It was all in those dreams. She was taking their power away just like she used to let Sally take hers.

And wonderfully, the detectives deflated right before her eyes. Their chests sank and their chins fell as if they were a couple of those blow-up punching bags for kids. She almost felt sorry for them, all the energy they'd just expended. For nothing.

"But listen, thanks for buying my book," Angela said to them as she was walking out the door. "You guys bought more copies last week than I've sold since it was published."

The day after Helen had begun to clean his paintbrush as she so charmingly referred to their renewed sexual relationship, Jerome went to the health food store and filled his cart with apples and melon and broccoli and free-range chicken and active cultures yogurt and firm tofu and miso and green tea. He felt at peace with the world and in love with his body, that superior African love temple. It was amazing how he'd changed since the old days when he used to be offended by her oral habits.

He was humming to himself as he passed through the homeopathic herbal aromatherapy section of the store. They were playing a tuneless instrumental piece but Jerome didn't care if he sounded like an ass. He picked up some crystal deodorant (no toxic aluminum) and some baking powder toothpaste. He didn't need any herbal/homeopathic Viagra, that was for sure.

When he got home, after he put everything away in the refrigerator and cupboards, after he sat down with a cup of Tranquility Tea, he decided to try to get in touch with his feminist intellectual daughter. He'd tell her he was wrong about testifying as the defense team's expert witness in that case about the rapist. He'd assure her he never worked with criminals anymore, particularly the ones who preyed on women.

And if that wasn't enough he'd tell her all about the scandal at Maryfield Academy and about Angela and even about the chapbook, *HeartMurder,* that she'd written under that pseudonym. The one he'd gotten her to sign. He'd always suspected that Suzanne was a lesbian (with a crummy mother like Stella who wouldn't still be looking for intimacy with a woman?) and now that he could build a bridge to her through poetry she'd have to be impressed.

Filled with new vigor after flattening the detectives, Angela skipped down the stairs out of Helen's office, out of the interview, and into the hot spring air. Kids were laughing, rushing along the hallway to lunch. Watching them, she surprised herself by missing Sister Rose James and her rabid squirrel-like presence hurrying kids along, checking their uniforms with her beady, busy eyes.

Where was she now? Shipped up north to the Mother House, Angela'd heard, in a straight jacket with one of those Hannibal Lecter masks on to keep her from taking a bite out of anybody else. That was the rumor anyway, substantiated by one look at Helen's beefy fore-arm with the huge bandage wrapped around it covering disinfected human tooth marks and twenty stitches. Maybe she'd try to write R. J. a letter just to let her know somebody cared.

"Ms. Martin?" somebody said. It was Alice Todesco, the new stu-dent with the penis dream in her modern novels class.

"What?" Angela said, none too warmly. They were standing in the doorway of her classroom, Alice leaning against the door, looking pale and needy.

"I wanted to know when Ms. Hamington is coming back," she said.

"You miss her, do you?" Angela said. A clear crush case if she ever saw one. It was hard to believe anybody could be enamored of Sally, even pasty Alice. "Well, come on in."

"I have something for her," Alice said, bending her head and taking a seat at one of the desks.

"She'll return as soon as some personal things get settled." Angela said with as much sympathy as she could muster.

Alice began to fumble around in her backpack. Finally she pulled out a spiral notebook.

"Here," she said. Inside she'd found an envelope with *Ms. Sally Hamington* typed on the front. Angela gasped. It looked exactly like the one she had found on her desk a few months before. The one about pedophilia.

Walt knew it was irrational to be so afraid of Sally. She'd explained how she hadn't even put her hands around his throat, how his faint was from intense emotion. She'd examined her fatal flaw, her need for control, her demand that everybody do things her way. In fact, she'd even started letting Blackie sleep on their bed. She stopped folding her underwear and alphabetizing the canned goods.

Still, when she started talking about how she was going to get her job back, he began to worry. The planning and obsessional thinking, the fire she'd get in her eyes, got him actually imagining that she might try to strangle him again.

"Sally," he said. They were lying in bed, watching *The X-Files,* her favorite show, and eating messy Fritos and salsa, her idea, something she'd never let them do before she'd examined her flaw and tried to remedy it.

"Yep," she said. "What?" She was annoyed. He was interrupting her show.

"I think you should get another job. Let Maryfield go. They're never going to solve the crime. You've got to move on."

Very slowly she turned to face him, her expression impassive, stony, scary.

"What makes you think any school will hire me after the kind of recommendation Helen's going to give? I'll have to work as an aide in a stinking nursing home or the dog pound putting animals to sleep all day long."

She was shaking with the impotent rage she'd kept stored up all month while she was trying to be mellow and loose for him.

He did exactly the right thing. He pushed her down and began to make love to her. He was rough and athletic which worked just fine in taming her creepy energy. But he knew he wasn't going to be able to jump her every time she got mad. In fact, now that they were together so much and she was acting so strange, sex with her wasn't really all that good. And he didn't even want to think about what might happen the next time he pissed her off.

So after she fell asleep he sneaked into the kitchen and dialed David Brand, the psychologist whose name a friend at his part-time job had given him. Walt didn't have any idea what he was going to say. He figured he'd come up with something when the answering machine clicked on.

"Hello," David Brand answered. It was the real guy, not a tape.

"Help me," Walt said melodramatically. He hadn't had time to figure out anything else.

"Who is this?" David said.

"Walt Hamington, and I'm afraid of my wife."

It wasn't as bad as R. J. thought it would be being shipped off to the Mother House. She was actually kind of a celebrity among the sisters for having taken a bite out of Helen's arm. One old nun, Sister Mary Frederick, slapped her on the back and said, "Good for you," as if R. J. were an addled saint like Joan of Arc, doing misunderstood, eccentric feats of courage for the good of God. The main thing was that Helen hadn't pressed charges. R. J.'s superior promised to have her seek psychotherapy.

Which somehow everybody seemed to forget once she was settled in, sans Prissy, who'd kindly been adopted by a teacher at Maryfield. Animals were forbidden because too many old nuns died at the Mother House leaving their pets behind. Maybe that was enough punishment, R. J. thought, having to give up her cat. Maybe that's why they forgot to send her to the doctor.

They did let her bring her computer with her. She had her own room with plenty of electricity and even a phone line so that part of her life was just fine. All she had to do was to make bread three days a week and help the retired sisters make their beds and do their laundry, so she had plenty of time to get back to the chat rooms.

The only difference was that this time she wasn't Mona, the sex-starved nun who told racy stories to demented lapsed Catholics. This time she was Robin, who, for lack of a more precise description, was the online mouthpiece for God Himself, or Herself, depending on your point of view. The Mother Superior and the other sisters hadn't the faintest idea that R. J.—Robin—was channeling God for the masses from her tiny monastic cell. Most of them weren't computer literate. Several of them were legally blind. All R. J. told them was that she was spreading God's word, which was technically accurate, although the word she was spreading wasn't the word of any Roman Catholic God they knew.

"Is it safe?" the Mother Superior asked her one afternoon in the huge convent kitchen which was much too big for the shrinking number of nuns now in residence. Rose James was slamming soft bladders of dough onto the marble counter with more energy than Mother Mary Rita had seen anybody expend in ages. She wasn't used to someone of R. J.'s relative youth around the house.

"Is it safe?" R. J. repeated. "What do you mean?"

"Well, do people know they're talking to you?" Mary Rita wasn't being intrusive exactly. She was actually rather diffident, the way the technologically illiterate often are in the face of some machine they don't understand. "And what if somebody out there doesn't like what you have to say?"

R. J.'d designed a Web site, www.Robingod.com., where she explained God's attitude toward human behavior (everything except activities that hurt others was acceptable in His/Her eyes), forgiveness (unintentional hurt was redeemable), and Catholic Girls' Schools (those who live in glass houses, etc.). She maintained a chat room and she had begun renting a P.O. box in town. All costs were paid for through donations that followers insisted on sending in. Never once had she solicited and she already had $900 in the bank. People sent her notes and photographs so she'd have someone to focus on when she channeled the Lord on their behalf, but she never told them who she was. They didn't seem to want to know.

"It's not a concern, Mother. I'm using a pseudonym and I never mention anything about the order at all. Just God, and Her/His good words." R. J. began to form the dough into four loaves of sunflower whole grain bread, a recipe she'd picked up on the Internet. R. J. could have afforded to buy the convent a breadmaker from Robingod's growing bank account, but she figured that using her hands to feed the flocks was yet another way of being close to her maker.

"Well, all right then, dear," Mother said. "And your bread certainly smells heavenly." R. J. beamed and sliced her a fresh piece from the loaf that had just come out of the oven.

"I have God's assurance that my work on the computer is penance for all the trouble I caused back at Maryfield," she said handing the Mother Superior the warm bread. "I hope I have yours."

But Mother either didn't hear the question or didn't care to answer because all she did was stand in the middle of the kitchen chewing on the sweet brown bread and humming so softly R. J. could hardly hear the tune.

Who would have guessed that biting Helen's arm would turn out to be the big break she was looking for in her life, sending her to the Mother House faster than if she'd been fired for incompetence or if she'd been diagnosed with some terminal illness. Now the only orders she had to follow were God's.

And not only had the bite sent her to the Mother House, it had motivated her to find the best bread recipe she could. Should she admit to her inspiration? That bite she'd taken out of Helen's arm was so soft, so satisfying, she had spent the past few weeks trying to recapture its flavor. A kind of cinnamon vanilla or honey wheat or was it this latest, molasses with raisins? And after she found the perfect taste she might look into creating wafers for the convent communion host. R. J. smiled and slapped another lump of dough on the marble counter; it was all so moving how God worked once you really let Him do His thing.

Angela decided that the best way to deal with the psychic pressure of being the prime suspect in the Sally Hamington harassment and attempted murder case was to figure out who did it herself. And now that she had Alice Todesco's note to Sally in her hand she had a good idea where to begin.

After school she called Erin and Megan de Cervantes to her room for a little talk. She'd noticed them during her lunch surveillance darting in and out of bathrooms and yet never using the toilets. She noticed the way they sat down with girls who weren't in their classes and twice she thought she heard the name "Hamington" whispered when they were around.

Finally, as the bell rang to signal the end of lunch, when she caught them going through the wastebasket in the Xerox room, she knew she'd found what she was after: insider detectives, silent sleuths probably assigned to the case by their mother, the school lawyer, to find out information nobody else could get.

She was right. They admitted it immediately. Angela was an adult and a teacher and thus deserving of the truth, although they had ascertained from their investigation that because she and Sally didn't get along, she might be a suspect herself.

They sat in student desks, wearing perfectly pressed gray pleated skirts, their long legs discreetly crossed at the ankle. Angela stood to emphasize a power differential she didn't feel, facing their beady black eyes, straight sharp bangs, and teeth sparkling behind expensive metal orthodonture.

"We couldn't help but pick up some talk about you," Erin or Megan said, but not nastily. They were smart kids, too smart for snap, circumstantial judgments, a lot smarter than Rex and Chuck. They were doing their job without an ax to grind.

"In that case, you'll understand why I'm interested in your findings. I'm annoyed that I'm being tied to this case simply because Ms. Hamington and I had differences. I want you to help me find the real perpetrator."

"Of course," Megan said. "We've been expecting you to contact us ever since the detectives interviewed you. We understand your interest in solving the case. We can't really comprehend why you'd have differences with Ms. Hamington though. But 'chacun à son goût' as they say in France."

Angela laughed. These two were something else.

"What do you charge for your services?" she asked.

Erin whipped out a pocket calculator and did some fast figuring.

"Expenses, overhead, per diem," Megan said. "Will $25 a day work for you?"

"Deal," Angela said. "But you have to keep it quiet, even from your mother. I'm sure you understand."

They looked at each other. This was a big moment. This was difficult. They'd always told their mother everything.

"Excuse us," Erin said. Angela walked to her blackboard and began to erase an old lesson about *Oedipus Rex* while they conferred.

"OK, Ms. Martin," Megan said. "Because this is a professional situation we believe our mother would understand the ethical need for confidentiality." And then the three of them solemnly shook hands.

"I want you to start with Alice Todesco," Angela said. "Work your way into her life and then tell me what you find there. I want you to do it fast."

"Not Sheila Campbell?" Erin said. "We've got some nice information about her and Hamington and a late term paper."

"Erin," Megan pointed at the big poster on the wall and then grabbed her sister's hand. "Let's go make friends with Alice before she leaves campus. Maybe she'll offer us a ride home. Ours is not to question authority." And with that the two of them left the room.

Helen was sitting in front of her largest canvas yet, contemplating the composition she'd been working on all day. It was late afternoon on a Sunday and she was pooped. But good pooped, not bad pooped the way she'd felt during most of the Sally Hamington/Rose James thing. In fact, just this weekend she'd realized that she was happy again, in a new way from before the crisis actually: freer, deeper, wider. She'd decided to stretch her biggest canvas ever and paint something on it to express her joy.

She was wearing an old caftan, one she'd picked up in Zimbabwe during the trip she'd taken with her mother five years ago. She loved the damn thing, the way it tented out over her mountains and rivers and rolls of flesh gently and with acceptance instead of in the punishing way the tight dresses and suits she had to wear all week made her feel. She lit a cigarette and took a deep drag. This was the real Helen Blalock, this big beautiful zaftig painter of large canvases and she had the stupid mess at Maryfield to thank for all of it.

Jerome Brooks was asleep near her feet, curled up like a big dog, a good dog, on the mattress she used as a couch in her studio. She had Maryfield to thank for Jerome coming into her life again. He had a perfect right to be pooped, too. They'd made love for three hours this morning after he arrived with coffee and bagels. And this time they'd gone all the way, which had made her feel loosy-goosy and earth-mothery, not violated at all. She'd contained him; he hadn't penetrated her; she'd sat astride him, which wasn't the least awkward because he was a big man, 6'3" at least and maybe 250 pounds. And she was big, God knew, so they looked right together if anybody'd been looking.

The painting needed work of course but the main outline was there— landscape as woman—not in the ugly way Georgia O'Keeffe painted it, those stupid pastel floral labia things or hard desert landscapes. Georgia obviously hated both women and nature which is the reason she changed everything into an idea and bent the landscape to fit her own vision. Helen's work wasn't like that; the mountain looked like a silhouette of her body: hips, buttocks, shoulders, but like a mountain, too, so that the viewer could take it however they wanted. Beauty was the important thing, after all.

Jerome was snoring softly. This morning he'd told her he wanted to move in and support her while she painted. He wanted her to quit her job. He wanted her to meet his daughter Suzanne with whom he'd just reconnected, who seemed to know Angela Martin from several years before.

She looked down at him fondly. Maybe she'd let him spend the night this time. They could sleep on the mattress in here, near her painting, so that she could add to it whenever she felt the urge or dreamed of an image she wanted to capture right then. She'd paint in the nude, in the moonlight and maybe she'd call school in the morning, call in sick, for the first time since she took the job, just because she could.

Alice had missed exactly three appointments with David Brand, which was probably why she'd blurted out the penis dream in Ms. Martin's novels class. Her father was out of town, in Paris on business, so nobody cared if she canceled. He'd asked her what she wanted him to bring her back from his trip, like she had a clue what was for sale there that was different from here. When he'd gone to Cairo, he'd said, "What can I bring you back from Cairo?" Alice had no idea what was in Egypt except pyramids so he brought her one, a rose crystal pyramid that you could see through in the right light. All she could think of from Paris was the Eiffel Tower.

Erin and Megan de Cervantes told her she was a dope.

"Of all the things he could bring you from Paris and you say a monument. He'll bring you a metal lamp or something."

"What should I have said?" They were in Alice's frilly room trying on her mother's clothes, the stuff she'd made her father let her keep after she died. Her mother had been tall and slender, like the twins, so it made sense especially because the girls could use them in the fancy places they went like restaurants and theaters and Paris.

"Well, clothes for one thing and of course jewelry. You should always ask for jewelry. He'll get you something valuable which you can sell later if you don't like it."

The reason Alice had missed her appointments with David was because she had been spending all her time with the twins, learning whatever they felt like teaching her, mainly things she'd never get at Maryfield about being rich and spending money. Since she first met them looking for a ride home after school she'd stopped cutting herself almost completely. The scars on her legs and feet were thin white lines now, more like wrinkles than scars.

"So when did you stop cutting yourself?" Erin said.

"What?" she said hoping maybe she'd heard wrong, that Erin had maybe said, "Doubting yourself."

"You heard me, slicing at your skin."

"Awhile ago," Alice said. "I don't know why."

"Why you did it or why you stopped?"

"Either one." She couldn't tell them the truth, that she did it when she felt bad inside and that the two of them had made her feel so much better and less lonely, even though they were two years younger, that she didn't need to do it anymore. She couldn't tell them she wanted to go places with them and their mother, Theresa, or maybe trick their parents into getting married like in *Parent Trap*. And she certainly couldn't tell them about what she'd done to Ms. Hamington, with a little help from her crushed-out neighbor Jeremy, the one who doctored her grades for $250 whenever she asked him. This time she'd paid him $500 for nothing. The thing had backfired so completely that she wouldn't even speak to him anymore. The thing had backfired so bad that Ms. Hamington was gone for good.

David had been seeing Walt Hamington for three weeks (he'd scheduled him for Alice's evening hour temporarily) before Walt finally got up the nerve to ask, haltingly, breathlessly, yet still trying to appear offhanded:

"Are you by any chance homosexual? It doesn't matter of course. My cousin is, my high school running coach, my college fraternity brother. I just wondered out of curiosity. Don't answer if you don't want to. Doesn't matter in the least one way or the other. Homosexuality is genetic anyway. You can't help it. You're born that way, aren't you? I don't mean 'you' of course, I mean 'one.' Just like I was born heterosexual." Walt paused finally looking all pink and heated up.

"So if it doesn't matter, why do you want to know?"

"It's interesting, that's all. People interest me," Walt said.

"Well then, yes, I am," David said. "What made you guess?"

"Everything. Your manner, your size."

"Fit the stereotype, do I?" David said.

"Don't be angry. I don't think of you as a stereotype or some pervert just because other people do. Just because you people get beat up outside bars, lampooned on TV, and targeted with responsibility for the tragedy of AIDS. You're the victim, not the cause. Small-minded uneducated people blame you for their own problems." Now Walt was gesturing at David, pointing and jabbing in a peculiar way.

"Walt, Walt," David tried to sound calming and paternal although he didn't feel that way at all. He felt angry and vaguely frightened. These straight men were so goddamn afraid of being near a faggot you didn't know what they'd do. He sure as hell wasn't going to reach out and pat him on the knee.

"What?" Walt said, pulling himself together.

"Does any of this sound familiar?"

There was a long pause while Walt considered the question. David waited, listening to the cars outside, birds, voices, air-conditioning hum. Then he began to think about the e-mail that he had discovered from Eduardo, the critical-care nurse, to Tony, his Tony, last night, mentioning dinner, signed love. He thought about the best method for confronting Tony, and then, after that, about living alone in a house overlooking the lake with a dog, where he'd spend quiet evenings reading Gore Vidal in front of the fire.

"Yes," Walt said finally.

"OK, yes," David said. "Go on."

"Sally, my wife, of course, and her being tied up and harassed and then blamed for it all which is the last thing anybody should do. But . . ."

"But what?" David said gently.

David had already recognized Sally as a teacher Alice admired at Maryfield Academy but he hadn't broken confidentiality to tell Walt, who was beginning to get all pink and agitated again. This was evidently dangerous territory. He didn't know exactly what he was getting into. He'd used one of the stock questions about emotional issues being interconnected like he always did after a client went off on an unrelated tangent, just fishing for associations, and now he'd come up with something more complicated than he'd bargained for.

"But I do blame her. I blame her for everything. I do, I do, I do."

David watched him weep. He knew not to jump in and try to make him feel better. That much was obvious. It wasn't that David was really tempted to do anything anyway. He was always fascinated by the moment someone's emotions got the better of them, at the moment of breakthrough. It was as though the alien hiding inside had popped out and had begun to tell the real truth finally, in spite of the patient, in spite of the therapist, too.

After awhile he said, "We have a few more minutes if you'd like to talk."

Walt nodded and took a Kleenex off the table. "Thanks," he said. "It seems so clear now."

"Explain."

"My relationship with Sally. Why I was attracted to her. How I embraced her strength, her focus, as my own. How I essentially lost myself in her, submerging my own needs and identity to elevate hers. I've become a child."

"Will the relationship allow for change?" David said. He held Walt's eyes for a moment to allow the question to sink in. He suddenly noticed that they were very, very blue.

He also noticed that, late as it was, he didn't feel the least bit sleepy.

After reassuring him that he wasn't looking at all homosexual, a fear he'd secretly harbored ever since his interview with Sister Rose James when she'd implied he did, Sophy asked Chuck to come to bed with her. This time she asked him to be a priest which he thought was truly bizarre given the fact that she was Jewish. And, on top of that, weren't a lot of priests homosexual? He'd gladly been a girl, a Labrador retriever, and her great-grandfather in recent months, but a priest? What was that?

"Are you sure you don't mean Rabbi?" he'd asked her.

"What is this?" she said. "You being anti-Semitic again? Can't Jews fantasize about priests?"

"How can I be anti-Semitic when I'm Jewish?" he asked.

"You tell me," she said.

"Maybe it's that damn Maryfield job getting to me. Priests, nuns, crucifixes, secrets, and I can't seem to get a handle on who's behind it. Every time I'm sure I've fingered the perp, the lead evaporates or seems ridiculous. I'm not even sure if it's a teacher, a student, or Sally herself."

"Has anything happened since she's been banned?" Sophy asked, lying naked and ready between the sheets.

"Not a peep. Not a note. Nothing." he said. "Which doesn't tell me a thing."

"Except that it's over. That's the point isn't it?" Sophy said, reaching under the sheets to grab him. It was time to start. She had an early day tomorrow.

"Not if you're Sally Hamington wanting her job back and wanting revenge," he said. And then he rolled over on top of her. "Not if you're Sally Hamington, my child."

"Oh, Father," Sophy moaned. "Forgive me."

The next morning Chuck met with Helen in her office to tell her that as far as he was concerned, the case was over.

"You're kidding," she said.

He moved uncomfortably in his chair. He could hardly breathe with the smoke and all her decorative crap all over the surfaces in the room. And Helen was getting so fat. Since he'd been on the case, she must have gained fifty pounds. Not that he was judgmental about womens' weight. They had a right to be as big as they wanted to be. Sophy wasn't small: C-cup breasts, size twelve jeans, and he never said a word about that. Whenever she asked him if her butt was too fat or if her breasts had begun to sag he always said no. He'd learned his lesson from that time he'd answered honestly, thinking she really wanted his opinion, when he'd said her butt did seem a little bigger. Jerome Brooks' interpretation of the perpetrator's psychology was totally lame: fear of large women. What that probably was was Jerome Brooks' own psychology, simple as that.

It was just that Chuck was beginning to feel trapped in this tiny room with Helen sitting across from him, waiting for him to explain that he had failed.

"Nope," he said. "I'm not kidding. I believe that it's pointless for you to spend any more money investigating something that for all intents and purposes has been settled."

"How can you say it's settled?" Helen said, scratching something that looked like blue paint off her hand. She had to be as ready to give up the investigation as he was. Probably she was just pretending to hedge for appearances' sake.

"No more disturbances since she's been off campus," he said. "That was the main goal, wasn't it? Besides, what more can we do when she refuses to call in the police or look at a lineup or at any pictures? She destroyed evidence by washing her clothes after the 'incident' with the masked gunman. I think we're off the hook, Helen. I think we can go home on this one."

She thought about it for a moment.

"So I won't renew her contract at the end of the school year," she said finally. "You'll explain this to the Board?"

"Absolutely," Chuck said. He leaned back in his chair. He felt more expansive all of a sudden. God, he'd disliked Sally Hamington with all her superiority and not-so-hidden aggression. In a way, he didn't blame the perpetrator at all. But, all the same, he did hate to give up on a case. Made him feel like a damn loser.

"You did a good job, Chuck," Helen said, "with what you had to go on. Rather thankless, wasn't it?"

"Frustrating as hell, to be perfectly honest. I'm actually thinking about closing my agency and going back to police work where I can use a bit more muscle to pry out the truth. My wife just told me her division is opening up a Hate Crimes Unit."

"I wonder if we'll ever find out what really happened and who was behind it all?" Helen said.

"Probably not," he said. "For once I have to agree with Jerome. Mostly the only time you ever know anything one hundred percent is on TV or in a mystery book. Not in real life, that's for sure."

Vincent Todesco was as nervous as a schoolboy. He hadn't had a blind date in twenty years and here he was, against his better judgment, on his way to pick up the mother of Alice's little twin friends, Theresa de- something.

"De Cervantes," Alice piped up from the backseat. "They're Italian, like we are. Isn't that perfect?"

"I think it's Spanish," Vincent said, but when he noticed in the rearview mirror that Alice was pouting, he corrected himself. "You're right, Italian. Like us."

How the hell had she gotten him to agree to this? Well, it didn't help his leverage any that she'd caught him doing Ginny, the housekeeper, the night before he left for Paris. Poor kid. What a sight to walk in on your old father getting laid.

"Don't bring me anything from Paris," Alice had told him long distance last week. "Just promise to take Erin and Megan's mother out to dinner when you get home. That's all I ask."

So he'd agreed. Plus it was harder still to refuse Alice anything when lying next to him in bed at the Le Grand Hotel was the most beautiful creature he'd ever seen, named Marie-Francoise. She looked exactly like a young, very young, Catherine Deneuve and her smooth skin had made his fingertips hum.

So all he had to do was take Theresa out to dinner and make nice conversation. He could do that. She was probably dreading the situation as much as he was, only doing it for the sake of the twins and a good meal. Alice had told him what a terrific gourmand the woman was. Besides, she was an attorney. Maybe he could get her to talk about tax law, get some free advice on a few business matters. He'd take the meal as a business expense. What was the harm in that?

"How's David?" he asked Alice now, looking at her in the rearview mirror again. She was more animated than usual, and, although he thought she was probably too old to be going through puberty, she seemed to have gotten somewhat more of a figure just since he'd been gone. He thanked God his mess with Ginny didn't seem to be having a lasting effect.

"OK, I guess," she said. "I haven't actually gone to therapy in three weeks."

"Really?" he said. Good. He'd had enough of David Brand for awhile. Did that mean she was getting well?

"Turn here," she said.

"Is that all right, that you haven't been going to see him?"

"I've stopped cutting, if that's what you mean," she said.

Maybe this wasn't such a bad idea about Theresa de Cervantes after all, Vincent was thinking. These twins seemed to be good for Alice. Maybe he'd give old Terry a whirl, even if she had to be at least forty to have kids around Alice's age. Maybe even, he found himself shocked as hell to be thinking, stopped at the signal in his Bentley, it was time for him to get married again.

Angela was sitting at home in the director's chair holding the letter Alice had given her for Sally Hamington. It was unopened. She was pretending to struggle with the decision but she knew she'd probably read it sooner or later. So what if opening a private letter was an immoral act? Alice was a suspect for God's sake.

Besides, after the shock of her ex-lover Suzanne calling last night out of the blue (Angela hadn't until then made the amazing and coincidental connection that her father was the forensic guy, Jerome Brooks), she was feeling too good to think twice about anything.

Suzanne had congratulated her on the sapphic chapbook her father had read to her over the phone (so proud, public, and poetic) and invited her out for dinner, undoubtedly realizing what a prize she'd dumped, finally.

Of course she would read the letter. Her ex-girlfriend wanted her back; her chapbook was selling. She'd do whatever she pleased.

Dear Ms. Hamington:
Everybody here at Maryfield misses you so much. You are the best teacher I've ever had even though I got bad grades and you thought I was stupid and lazy.

Angela had to laugh. She and Alice had more in common than met the eye.

Anyway, I want you to know that you were wrong. I'm not dumb at all. In fact, I keep a journal full of stories, poems, and artistic observations. And, for my future career, I am going to be a famous writer. Best wishes until we meet again,
Alice Todesco

Angela put the letter down. So Alice was trying to clear the air with Hamington. She had more guts than Angela did. She was kind of an inspiration, actually.

All of a sudden Angela decided to approach Helen about offering creative writing as a regular part of the program with herself as the instructor. In fact, just in case Sally didn't ever return, she was going to completely rewrite the English department curriculum to fit her own personal philosophy of education.

Angela put Alice's letter aside and began to jot down possible course titles:

Literature of the Irrational
Catastrophe Fiction: Holocaust, Apocalypse, and the Locust
Poetry of Coleridge, Rimbaud, Sappho, and Sexton (or Amy Lowell, Djuna Barnes, and Gertrude Stein)
Urban Mythology for the Millennium

On the last day of school before finals Angela asked Alice to stay after her class on Camus' *The Plague* to discuss a certain "matter important to them both." Then Angela taught the class, purposely emphasizing the existential and metaphorical subtext of the novel, just to watch Alice squirm.

"Evil overtakes a small community. Everyone reacts differently to the fear, but everyone reacts just the same. Religion, greed, sex, denial, and hope all eventually give way to the realization that the only thing that matters is today."

"What about love?" somebody called out. "I thought that was the main lesson Rieux taught. Love for fellow human beings in the face of despair."

"That was what got him through. But everybody else returned to their same old patterns of behavior once the crisis was past. That's a lesson, too."

"What do you think would happen here," Jessica Reynolds asked, "if some plague hit Maryfield?"

"Nothing as philosophical as in Oran. I think it would probably bring out the worst in everybody, even the people it killed, and then it would be over. As simple as that."

"I think you're wrong," Annie Klinestiver, the pregnant senior, said. "I think it would bring out the best in some, too."

"Maybe we're both right," Angela said. "Sometimes it's difficult to tell the difference between the two."

She glanced at Alice who was busy writing something in her notebook.

"Are you listening, Alice?" she said. Alice looked up, her face flushed.

"Yes, Ms. Martin," she said. "I've heard everything. 'Best, Worst. Can't tell the difference.' I'm taking notes." And then she bent her head back down toward her paper and started writing again even though nobody was saying a word.

The class had gone well, especially with Jessica's question about the plague at Maryfield. Angela couldn't have planned it better if she'd tried. And by the time it was over, Alice looked like she wanted to bolt.

"You've changed, Alice, since the beginning of the quarter," Angela said when it was just the two of them. And Alice had. Although she was acting terrified right now she was also much less mousy and she seemed to have grown.

"My hair, maybe," Alice said. On the advice of Theresa de Cervantes she'd gotten it cut short.

"Any more weird dreams?"

Alice winced. Angela was being deliberately provocative and a tiny bit mean but she wanted to see what was cooking inside Alice's strange little brain. Also, after what she'd done, the kid deserved it. She deserved to fry.

"You mean like the penis dream? No. From then on I haven't remembered anything."

"I've been thinking we needed to talk," Angela said. She was sitting at her desk and Alice was standing in front of her. "Please, sit down."

"Me, too," Alice said, taking a seat. That was a surprise. "I can't seem to find my journal. I wondered if maybe I'd left it in here. The cover is bears and angels although I'm thinking of changing that. It seems too childish now."

"Is this it?" Angela said, picking up the notebook from underneath some other papers. "I believe you left it in my classroom last week."

"Yes," Alice said, grabbing for it.

Angela pulled it back. She hadn't found it in her classroom. The twins had brought it to her, swearing they hadn't read it; that they'd only looked inside to see that it was what she had asked for. On a whim she'd asked them to keep an eye out for the journal Alice had mentioned in her letter to Sally. When they found it hidden under Alice's bed the very next day, Angela thanked them for their work and terminated their employment, paying them and swearing them to secrecy one last time.

"Before I return it," she said. "I wanted to tell you how inventive I found your entries about Ms. Hamington to be. How imaginative your description of saving her from the masked gunman was, for example. And how I think I finally understand your dream about the penis. Remember Alice, how you discovered upon analysis that 'pen is wrong'?"

"You read it? You read my private book?"

In the book, Alice had written a florid description of her plan for releasing Ms. Hamington from the dangerous Jeremy by breaking into the room through the unlocked door, squirting pretend pepper spray into the gunman's eyes, and pushing him out into the night screaming in pretend pain. Then, after being untied, Sally was supposed to fall into Alice's arms and whisper such corny words of gratitude that Angela had actually laughed out loud when she read them.

"Do you have any idea, dear Alice, how close you are to being put into reform school for what you've done? How close you are to having a criminal record that will follow you your whole life? Have you thought about what your daddy will think when he finds out how his daughter has used her expensive private school education? And worst of all, what Ms. Hamington will think about what you've done to her life?"

Alice blanched and then recovered enough to talk.

"My friend—ex-friend—Jeremy screwed up," she said. "He heard some noise outside and ran off before I could perform the rescue. The rest is history. She's never coming back now, is she?"

"I heard that the principal didn't renew her contract," Angela said. "Would you like her to return?"

"How could she?"

"Isn't it obvious? All we have to do is tell Ms. Blalock and the detectives about your activities. Ms. Hamington wouldn't be in danger anymore if they knew you'd orchestrated everything, the letters, the pretend suicide. But, naturally, that would be the end of you."

Alice began to twirl a strand of short hair around her finger.

Then she began to cry; large, sloppy tears rolled down her cheeks.

"Which isn't to say that I'm not impressed by your nerve and your stealthy maneuvers. I'm not even going to ask how you got all those letters into the faculty mailboxes."

"I wanted her to notice me," Alice whispered. "I wanted to be valuable when I made it all end."

"And how were you going to do that?"

"I hadn't really worked that out, but somehow the letters were just going to end. Maybe because the writer gave up after Ms. Hamington got saved."

"One last thing, Alice," Angela said. "How did you know the word 'pedophile'? I don't think Maryfield has that on its vocabulary lists."

"I'm not lazy and I'm not dumb," Alice said, as if reciting a mantra. "Ms. Hamington thinks I am but she's wrong."

"Of course she is," Angela said gently. She couldn't help it. Alice was reminding her so much of herself. "I know that from your work in my class. You're very creative. You're going to be an excellent writer."

Alice looked at her, surprised.

"I am?" she said.

"Absolutely," Angela said. "Although I think your poetry could use some work." She opened the notebook and began to read:

> She takes my nipple into her mouth; it drives her wild.
> After she bites it she corrects my grammar.
> I want to hit her over the head with a hammer.

Alice covered her ears. "What now?" she said.

"That's up to you."

"It is?" she said. She wiped her face with a Kleenex. "You're not going to tell on me?"

"No, I'm not going to tell on you," Angela said.

"Why not?" Alice was looking at her with such profound and fawning gratitude Angela almost felt like she was acting with authentic compassion.

"Because I don't think it would do you a bit of good."

Angela had no idea what would happen to Alice if she did give the information to the detectives, if she'd be sent to some detention hall or mandatory volunteer work or thrown out of school. Maybe she'd be trundled off to Jerome Brooks for rehabilitation which, according to Suzanne, would be worse than a joke.

"I'll do anything."

But that wasn't the real reason. Angela didn't care about the quality of the rehab and she didn't care what Daddy would think. She didn't care about Alice Todesco in the least.

The real reason she'd decided not to tell anyone about the identity of the perpetrator in "the Sally Hamington case" was because Alice had done her work for her as surely as if Angela had been pulling the strings herself.

It was a clear, breezy graduation day at Maryfield for which Helen Blalock was deeply grateful. The weather channel had been predicting rain and since the school didn't have an auditorium, rain would have put them in the dingy cafeteria where pillars made the sight lines terrible.

But the day was perfect and all the teachers looked happy and relaxed. Final exams had been graded, report cards filled out, lockers cleaned, and she had just learned that enrollment for the next school year had actually gone up in spite of the Sally Hamington scandal.

Amazingly, contract talks had come and gone without incident. Sally hadn't even called. A few weeks afterward Helen got the news that Sally had taken a job at a struggling inner-city Catholic High School where the principal hadn't even bothered to check her credentials. Maybe the Maryfield community could forget all the unpleasant things that had happened and move on resolutely into the new millennium.

That would be the theme of her brief remarks today: "Maryfield, a school for the new millennium—where love of learning, of teaching, and of the truth will be the order of the day."

She was sitting on a raised platform with the Board of Trustees and the faculty, looking over the heads of the graduating seniors who were facing the audience of parents and friends. Annie Klinestiver was sitting in the back row, her enormous pregnancy hidden under the disposable white gown all the girls were wearing. Although she was technically valedictorian and should have been giving the commencement address, Helen had prevailed upon her to step down and allow Sheila Campbell, salutatorian, to give the speech, titled: "Maryfield Academy, Beacon of Light in an Unknowable Future."

Sally Hamington, no longer banned from campus, was sitting in the audience staring straight ahead. Alice Todesco, a little to her left, one row behind, hadn't taken her eyes off her once during the entire ceremony. It was all very familiar, the watching and not being seen, but this time Ms. Hamington looked somehow smaller than she had before. For a moment, Alice felt proud of what she'd been able to pull off. Lately she'd begun to think of the whole business in a new way; she almost felt proud. And she didn't miss Sally Hamington anymore at all. In fact, making her have to leave Maryfield, even if it had been unintentional, was no slight feat and to do it without being discovered (except by Ms. Martin) was pretty amazing. Alice smiled. What power! What a secret!

To Angela, who had noticed Sally while she was scanning the crowd during Helen's boring speech, she looked tragic, the way those who have fallen far and fast tend to look. It didn't help that she was so tall and had seemed so invincible. Like a felled redwood Sally Hamington sat in the audience grieving for her lost place among the Maryfield faculty, friendless, humiliated, defeated. Angela almost felt like she would miss her.

Sally was listening carefully to Helen's speech. She was trying to learn from it how to give a public address and say so little that nobody, not one soul, would remember what had been said. Already she was certain she would soon be running the struggling high school that had given her the job sight unseen. Already she had plans for what she would do once she was principal and delivering controversial speeches wasn't part of it.

"Education has always been about the search for the truth. Giving our students the skills to find that truth is what Maryfield and its faculty and administration and staff is all about. Together, heads held high, we enter the new millennium, searching with love and honor for nothing less than that. And now I ask you to join us in the alma mater: 'Maryfield, we strive to . . .'"

Sally had stopped listening. She had it all figured out. Four years max and she'd be running the new school, giving motivational speeches about personal responsibility, self-esteem, and the importance of having a dream. Five years and she'd be attending principals' meetings with Helen Blalock or her successor. Ten years, her struggling inner-city school would be profiled on *60 Minutes* as an inspiring example of tough intelligent leadership in a challenging environment. Eleven and she'd be on the cover of *Time*.

Graduation was over. Sally stood up to leave with the rest of the crowd.

And then Serena and Gabe and their student helpers released 100 donated white helium balloons into the air to float above the heads of the graduates. Everybody turned their faces up to the sky to follow them. For a moment there was silence as all of Maryfield watched the white specks slowly disappear into the clouds as if there had never been any balloons at all.

ABOUT THE AUTHOR

Carla Tomaso has written several novels and collections of stories, including *The House of Real Love, Matricide,* and *Voyages Out.* She teaches high school English in southern California where she lives with Mary Hayden and their dogs, Ramsay and Biscuit. Recently, she and her writing partner, Maureen Linehan, adapted *Maryfield Academy* into a screenplay.